SHADES of CHAMELEON

SHADES of CHAMELEON

JDANIELS

sepia

BET BOOKS

BET Publications, LLC
http://www.bet.com

SEPIA BOOKS are published by

BET Publications, LLC
c/o BET BOOKS
One BET Plaza
1900 W Place NE
Washington, DC 20018–1211

All Kensington Titles, Imprints, and Distributed Lines are available at special quantity discounts for bulk purchases for sales promotions, premiums, fund-raising, and educational or institutional use. Special book excerpts or customized print-ings can also be created to fit specific needs. For details, write or phone the office of the Kensington special sales manager: Kensington Publishing Corp., 850 Third Avenue, New York, NY 10022, attn: Special Sales Department, Phone: 1-800-221-2647.

BET Books is a trademark of Black Entertainment Television, Inc. SEPIA and the SEPIA logo are trademarks of BET Books and the BET BOOKS logo is a regis-tered trademark.

ISBN: 1–58314–376–9

First Printing: June 2004
10 9 8 7 6 5 4 3 2 1

Printed in the United States of America

This one is for my mother and father.

ACKNOWLEDGMENTS

Special thanks to: Glenda Howard, Linda Gill, and all of the BET family. My agent, Sara Camilli. My family and friends who encouraged me throughout this project. Thanks to my fellow authors who encouraged me by watching their talent and wanting to be like them. Thanks to my fans who have embraced me.

There are no masks with depth so deep
As to hide the soul within . . .
Only the outer aliases . . .
Like a Chameleon changing skins . . .

SHADES *of* CHAMELEON

PROLOGUE

Brooklyn, New York

Margo Hunter stood quietly watching her reflection in the full-length mirror that connected to the back of her bedroom door. This case had been extremely chaotic from the start, but it was one that she had no doubt she could pull off. At least that's what she thought when she first got involved. She pulled her hair back in a ponytail, and then loosened it again, allowing her tresses to fall just below her shoulders. Stress lines were visible on her face. Tiredness also showed in her deep green eyes. Sighing deeply, she decided she would shower, change, and then get on with her unsettling assignment.

Minutes later as she dried herself from her shower, her cell phone rang.

"Hello?"

"I'm downstairs."

"Senator Mitchell?"

"Yes, it's me." He sighed. "Agent Hunter, I'm not so sure about this, and I hate getting the FBI involved, but I don't know where else to turn."

"Listen, we'll talk when you get to my room, okay? Believe

me, Senator, you're doing the right thing. We'll make sure that you are protected. So please don't worry."

"Okay," he said, swallowing. "I'll be up in two minutes."

After hanging up the phone, Margo sat quietly thinking about the situation that was unfolding. Never in her wildest dreams had she thought when taking this job she would be addressing the one and only Senator Alan Mitchell. Never did she think that her investigation of an escort/dance, drug palace would be twisted and smothered with murder, dirty politicians, and soon-to-be scandal. But she knew that scandal is what it would amount to once all was uncovered. And all the money in the world would not protect the guilty culprits. She'd make sure of that.

A minute later a quiet knock at her door grabbed her attention. She opened it, smiling brightly at the dark brown eyes that looked back at her—eyes that had a mixture of worry and fear in them. Senator Mitchell was a tall black man, with a full head of peppered gray hair.

"Hello, Senator," she whispered. "Please come in."

"Hello," he whispered back.

Looking around cautiously, he walked inside the apartment, taking off his dark brown suit coat once he seemed comfortable with his surroundings.

"Please, there's no one here but me."

"But how do I know you're not one of them?"

"You don't. But then again if you didn't trust me, would you have come here?" Margo asked, as she flicked a lighter, lighting her slim cigarette. She sat down on her rented beige sofa and gave Alan Mitchell a comforting look, hoping she could somehow calm him down.

Even though he was a man who had seen fifty a good ten years before, Margo could see that he had once been and still was a handsome man. Made her wonder why a man of his status and looks had to lower himself to having to buy sex.

"What made you go to an escort, Senator Mitchell? You have a wife, a good standing in the community, and people who trust you and believed in you when you got their vote."

"Are you here to judge me or to listen to my story?" he asked sarcastically.

Margo threw her hands up, with one of her blond locks flipping across her cheek as she spoke. "I'm sorry, definitely my bad. Why don't you tell me what happened from the beginning."

"Okay. They wanted me to change my vote."

"What vote? And who are they?"

"Michael Riley. The egotistical shit head set me up. And I know damn well David Huggins was behind it all!" he shouted. "They videotaped me with the whore."

"Benita James?" Margo asked. She had known Beebe well, and no matter her choice of occupation she was a good person. It definitely pissed Margo off that the senator was calling her a whore when he was the one who bought what goodies she had to sell. Margo swallowed back the wave of nausea that threatened to cause her to lose her dinner. Politicians made her want to puke.

"Benita was just as much a victim in this as you, Senator Mitchell, even more so since she is now dead. Wouldn't you agree?"

A knock at the door silenced their conversation.

"Were you expecting someone? You told me no one would know about this right now but you!"

"Shh! No one knows," Margo retorted. "Just hold up, okay?" *Good lord, he's antsy,* she thought to herself. She got up and looked out the peephole. There was a Domino's pizza man standing in the hallway. Opening the door slightly, she said, "Sorry, I didn't order a pizza."

As she was closing it again, she was suddenly flung halfway across the floor as a humongous weight pushed against the door. She looked up frightened as the pizza man pulled out a long-nosed semi. She moved her shaking body underneath the coffee table, gasping in horror as two other men who wore shades also came into view. Both pulled out huge, 9 milli pistols. Margo couldn't see Senator Mitchell, but she heard him clearly as he screamed out, "No!"

Four gunshots, muffled with a silencer, killed his screams. Looking from beneath the table as the senator fell backward against the couch, Margo slid from underneath and jumped quickly to her feet. She knew that with Senator Mitchell dead she would probably be next, and she'd be damned if she was going to go without a fight. She ran toward her bedroom, almost getting the door shut before it came crashing back open. Her heart thumping, Margo rolled over on her bed, rushing to get her pistol out of her holster. She grabbed it, and then felt a swift kick to her wrist, causing her to drop her gun. She pressed back against her bed when she felt the gunmen's weapon at her temple.

"Who are you?" she asked bravely, swallowing her fear. "What do you want?"

"Doesn't matter who I am," the guy said.

Margo looked past him to the two other guys, one in the pizza uniform, the other dressed all in black, sporting long dreads that came down to his shoulders.

She looked back into the shades that covered the eyes of the man whose gun bore into her temple.

"Beg," he stated. She looked at him questioningly. "I said beg, you bitch."

"Go to hell!"

"Ha, ha," he laughed. "Cool. Have it your way." He cocked his gun. "Say hi to Jesus for me . . ."

The man pulled the trigger.

1

Washington, D.C.

The round wooden table shook as the commanding agent Kyte Williams sat down angrily, startling all who congregated around it. He looked at both agents, one to the other, waiting silently for either to speak.

"Well? Do either of you have any plans to tell me what's going on here?" he asked. "Where exactly is Agent Hunter?"

Malcolm Johnson, who was a senior agent in the East Coast division, spoke up.

"That's just it, we don't know. Margo hasn't been in contact with anyone in over a week. We don't want to jump to any conclusions. Which is why I don't understand . . ." He looked accusingly at the other agent who sat with them. "I don't understand why you were bothered with all this. But believe me, sir, we have our people checking into things."

"You know Agent Hunter. Is it normal for her to go this long without contacting anyone?" Williams asked.

"No, it's not."

All eyes looked toward the feminine, yet firm voice coming from the doorway.

Agent Johnson sighed when he saw who it was. Kimberla

Bacon, code-name Chameleon. Better known as, at least to him, the biggest pain in the ass this side of the East Coast.

He noticed the huge smile that grew on Detective Williams's face at the sight of her. It was known that she was his pet. But pet or not, this was not Kimberla's case, therefore, it was none of her business.

"Kimberla," Williams said, "come on in. Although you know you aren't supposed to be interrupting like this." He winked, smiling at her in the process.

Kimberla came in, closing the door as she walked toward the desk. "You knew I would be here, Kyte, if it concerns Margo, that is."

"It's not your business, Kimberla!" Malcolm Johnson snarled.

Kimberla looked at him.

"Malcolm! It's been far too long, dear heart!"

"Not long enough," he spat back.

Kyte put a halt to their *nice* words. "Agent Johnson, you're excused." He looked at Agent Micah Latimer. "You, too, Latimer. I'll talk to you two about this later."

Malcolm gathered the folder he had placed on Kyte Williams's desk, then gave Kimberla a disgusted look.

There was no secret that there was no love lost between the two. It had all boiled down to Kimberla receiving the promotion that Malcolm felt was his. The fact that a woman had up-scaled him didn't make the slap in the face that he imagined he received even worse. But instead of feeding into his bitter jealousy, Kimberla chose to ignore it most of the time. She simply gave him a sugar sweet smile whenever he passed her way.

Short men like Malcolm Johnson usually have small balls, Kimberla thought as he passed by her, brushing her elbow roughly. She laughed aloud, causing Malcolm to look up—he was a good three inches shorter than her—with his flared nostrils expanding even wider. Kimberla had no time or patience for the obnoxious little man. She winked at him, then turned her attention toward Kyte Williams. Kyte shook his head at her, having watched their exchange.

"How long are you and Malcolm going to keep up this private battle?"

Kimberla's dark eyes widened innocently. "What battle? I don't have a problem with Malcolm. That's on him." She smiled as she took a seat in front of Kyte's desk. "I'm always professional, and always nice."

"Oh really?"

"Yeppers," Kimberla responded cheerfully.

Kyte smirked at Kimberla, unconvinced.

"Why are you here, Kimberla? I thought you were going on vacation?"

"And I still have my vacation planned. But you know how close Margo and I are. You also know I would want to be a part of finding out where she is and what has happened to her."

Kyte sighed, looking at Kimberla with a worried expression. She didn't have to guess what he was thinking. He thought Margo was dead, that was pretty obvious. But she refused to entertain the thought. She and Margo had been the best of friends ever since the two joined the Bureau eight years ago. Margo had been content to work as an undercover agent, whereas Kimberla was more ambitious. From day one she had set her goal and hadn't stopped until she reached it. Two years ago she finally got the promotion she coveted, special agent in charge of her division, and she loved every minute of it.

Minus the occasional mishaps and some prejudices against her, being that she was not only a female SAIC, but a black one at that, things were going pretty well. She still shook inside whenever she thought about the disaster that happened with the Tristan Jackson case a year before. It was a disaster that ended up revealing the dark side of one of the most talented and devoted agents in her division. Now that things had quieted down with the shock of that, the last thing Kimberla needed was to worry about Margo, her soul mate and sister of hearts.

Kyte Williams cleared his throat to grab her attention. Kimberla blinked, looking back toward him.

"Kim, you have to trust me to find Margo. You need this vacation, and I mean for you to get it. You don't need to involve yourself in this."

Kimberla was quiet as she walked over to the wide picture window that walled to the left of Kyte's desk. Kyte had one of the nicer offices in their building. It almost made Kimberla jealous. Her office was not a dump. But as she looked at the stony beauty that was Washington, D.C.—its monuments and historical, patriotic loveliness from the past testifying to her through the clear window—she wished she could switch spots with Kyte.

"Kim, are you listening to me?"

She looked over to Kyte. "Let me help in the investigation, please? I just want to know what's going on, Kyte."

"And you will. There is no way I would keep you in the dark with this. I know how close you and Margo were."

"Are," she insisted.

"Okay, *are*. But still—"

"Then let me help," she cut in.

"No, you need this time off." Kyte got up, grabbed her arm softly and lead her to his door. "Take it, Kim. Go see your father. Go boating with that tall, dark and handsome boyfriend you're hiding, or—"

"I'm not hiding Brandon from anyone." Kimberla laughed. "And he is *not* my boyfriend."

"Uh huh, then what is he?"

"He's my backscratcher, or you could call him my *friend* with benefits." She smirked.

"Well go get your back scratched for a few weeks, and give me a call later and I'll fill you in on what we come up with, okay?" He smiled when Kimberla's smirk turned back into a pout as she walked along with him outside of his office. "No pouting allowed, my friend. I have to go myself, but call me. I promise I'll keep you updated on everything."

"Okay, fine," Kimberla said flatly, as she headed out with him.

They walked past Kyte's secretary. He looked at her and

said, "Go on and take your lunch, Missy. I'll be back myself in about two hours."

Minutes later as she sat at her office desk, Kimberla's mind wouldn't stop racing. She was already on auto. *I have to do something,* she thought. She owed Margo a hell of a lot more than to go vacationing while she was missing, maybe hurt, captured in some horrid situation or worse.

She got up from her desk, and then glanced over at the wide mirror with golden arms that took residency on her office wall. Her reflection showed her determination. The person that was housed in her slim 5'11" frame was not one who could sit back and let anyone else get answers to questions she had. The cocoa-colored skin she wore was not that thin. She had to find Margo herself. A lightbulb went off in her head as her vacation plans were suddenly changed. She knew that Margo was in Brooklyn, New York. What Kimberla didn't know was much about the case that Margo was working. But she knew exactly where she could find that information.

Knowing that Kyte and his secretary had left his office, she grabbed her bag and headed out on her own.

Kimberla had always hated flying. And ever since the September 11 drama, she hated it even more. Still she knew she was lucky to be able to get a flight out at this late date even though it cost an arm and leg and she was trying to save up for her first house. This was pinching her already tight wallet pretty badly. Her salary was nowhere near the point that she would ever be rich. In fact, she didn't know any wealthy FBI agents.

As she waited near the departure terminal at Dulles airport, she thought about her conversation with her latest boo-friend, Brandon. He had been upset about her sudden plan to leave for vacation without getting to see her to say good-bye. He was getting a bit too clingy anyhow, she reasoned. Even though men had their place in her life, they were not a total necessity as far as she was concerned. Her appeal had definitely changed from high school and college. Back then men never noticed her. She was too tall, too skinny, too athletic, too dark, too everything. The present rage that black don't crack wasn't in style in the late 1980s and early 1990s. Light was in, and although she was not really dark skinned, she certainly wasn't the Vanessa Williams type.

Kimberla looked up, catching the eye of a white man whose eyes had not left her from the moment she sat down. She snickered to herself. Now even white men seemed to find her attractive. It was surely a new day.

Twenty minutes later, she sat comfortably in coach on a Boeing 747 en route to JFK airport. The captain had announced it would be a short thirty-minute flight. But that didn't ease the queasiness in her stomach. She decided to call her father and let him know her change of plans. At least she could close her eyes while talking to him and not think too much about a possible crash landing.

She dialed her father's number after connecting the air phone to the adapter in front of her. He answered in two rings.

"Daddy?"

"Kimmy, where are you?" her father asked. "I've been trying to call you all day."

"Well . . . you won't believe this, but I'm on a plane to New York."

There was a pause. She could guess what her father was thinking.

"Daddy, are you there?"

"You aren't coming, are you?" he asked. She could hear the sadness in his voice.

"No, you're wrong. I have to go to New York for a short while, but I still plan on coming to Maryland on my way back."

Kimberla bit her lip. She knew that her father thought she worked too hard. He had been trying to get her to come home for a very long time, and she hated disappointing him. But finding Margo was too important.

"When are you going to start putting your own well-being and your family ahead of your job, Kimmy?" he asked. "I knew that when you said you would spend three weeks here it was too good to be true."

"I'm sorry, Daddy." She sighed. "But this is really important. You know how much I miss you and Janet."

Janet was her stepmother. The two women had never been very close. It wasn't that Janet stood in the way of Kimberla and her father's relationship or that Kimberla didn't feel that Janet loved her father, because she did. Janet gave him the companionship he had needed ever since her mother died ten years ago. However, Kimberla couldn't stand seeing another woman taking control in the home where she had grown up, or sharing the bed with her father that she felt was only her mother's place. It was an inner issue that she knew she would have to deal with someday. But she had never really gotten over losing her mother.

She had planned to swallow her own selfishness and spend three weeks getting to know her new stepmother. And maybe getting back some of the closeness with her father that had slowly vanished.

"Kimmy, you have to start thinking about what's most important, daughter."

"Daddy, I know what's most important. Please try to understand, okay? And one more thing." She swallowed, imagining her father's response at her next words. "If anyone calls from the Bureau asking for me, will you tell them I'm staying there with you for vacation? It's very important."

"You want me to lie for you?"

She bit her lip. "Not lie. I will be there. I'm just taking the long route home."

"Kimmy, what kind of trouble are you in now?"

Seeing that she had to get out of this conversation and quickly, Kimberla pulled the air phone from her ear. Speaking loudly she said, "I have to go, Daddy. The phone is going dead. Don't forget what I said."

"Kimmy!"

"I can't hear you, Daddy. I'll call you when I get to my hotel. Bye!"

Hanging up quickly, she smiled and wondered just how ready New York City would be for Kimberla Bacon.

2

Bronx, New York

The heat of the day hadn't cooled by evening.

Having lived in Los Angeles for three years, one would think that Jacob White would be used to hot weather. But heat was one thing; heat mixed with humidity and funk was a different matter. He sat in his leased Ford Excursion, struggling to breathe. Taking a deep breath, Jacob looked down at his watch. Mario Lincoln was late. It shouldn't surprise him. That nigga was the type who felt that everyone had to live their life according to his timetable. He was da shit of the Bronx and Brooklyn—kingpin hellion of the streets. At least he thought so.

Jacob was working undercover, but not necessarily to snag Mister Street-kingpin. He had bigger fish to fry. He wanted the boss man, Michael Shawn Riley. For the past year he had been able to get up close and personal with him. Riley trusted him like he would trust his own brother; probably even more so, since Riley was suspected—with no proof of course—of ordering his own brother's murder two years before. Michael Riley was one scary snake. But for the moment he trusted Jacob. He thought Jacob was named Jonathon Simmons, which actually was Jacob's alias. He thought he had a twin match in his murderous drug schemes. And Jacob's great acting ability gave him a front-row window that was going to get him his stripes once he nailed Michael Riley. Michael Riley was not his only target. The FBI and DEA had gotten a tip, after years of tracing Riley's activities, that he had political connections that would totally rock the foundation of New York's illegal drug industry. They wanted to know about these connections, and that would take time. They needed someone to get inside the underground of things, and Jacob White was that someone.

Jacob's thoughts were disrupted as he noticed Mario's shining new Caddy pulling up. Jacob got out of his vehicle, stretching his aching legs that were cramped from the long wait. His 6'5" frame had a hard time adjusting no matter how big the car or truck he drove. Scratching his beard, he walked over to meet Mario.

"Took you long enough."

"I had some shit to do," Mario responded back.

"And I didn't?" Jacob said sarcastically.

Mario gave him a sideward look, and then winked. "Calm down, my brotha. It's payday. That is, as long as this nigga don't try to be shady. I hate these lil petty cash fuckas walking around trying to play big on the streets. Then when it's time to pay up you can't find their asses."

Jacob grunted in agreement while following Mario to a row house setup. The music was loud and hip-hopped down, leaving no doubt as to where the party was. A heavyset sista opened the door, letting out a puff of smoke as she said, "Y'all gots a invitation? We ain't letting no crashers up in here tonight, ya heard?"

"Girl, get your big, fat, non-English-speaking ass away from the door," Mario spat.

The big girl's eyes bugged. Her mouth twisted in an indignant scowl. "Oh no you didn't go there. Dre! Come here, Dre. This Negro gon' try to diss me. Dre!"

A thuggish-looking brotha came in the room. He mumbled something, although it was hard to make out since he also possessed a heavy accent. He didn't need to say much. He pulled out a baseball bat and was obviously planning to let it talk for him. As soon as Mario saw it he quickly pulled out his .38.

"Wha', nigga, wha'?" Mario said with a threatening voice.

Jacob put himself on alert. This was fast getting way out of hand as it always did with Mario. He wasn't sure what Mario enjoyed more, the money or getting a chance to pistol-whip the shit out of someone now and then.

The thuggish brotha put down his bat. "Mah bad," he crooned, smiling to reveal a mouth full of gold caps. The roomful of party people got quiet as they watched the showdown.

"Now I'm looking for Brick," Mario continued, .38 still in hand. "I know he's here. So whatcha wanna do?"

A short, skinny, light-skinned, identical version of the rapper Jay-Z walked out of the crowd. He smiled nervously. Jacob figured he had to be Brick.

"Hey, dawg. Wassup?"

"You know wassup," Mario responded back.

He nodded his head toward the door. Surprisingly, Brick followed behind both Mario and Jacob as the screen door flapped loudly behind them. Within seconds, the quietness of the row house was filled again with hip-hop music and people getting their groove on.

They were almost to Mario's Cadillac when he grabbed Brick, throwing him into the backseat roughly.

"Hey, take it easy, Mario," Jacob said.

He could tell this whole thing was getting more than ugly. Jacob had seen his share of ugly for the past year, but that gun pointed at Brick's back worried him. He couldn't sit there and allow someone to be murdered right before his eyes. He wasn't *that* undercover.

Mario ignored him as he jumped in the car beside Brick. Jacob got in the front. Brick started talking right away.

"I got your money, man. It ain't gotta be all like this. I got it, yo!"

"Then why da fuck you been trying to play me?" Mario shouted.

"I wasn't." Brick's voice seemed to be shaking. He reached

in his back pocket and pulled out a wad of money. "See? We straight, yo."

Mario snatched the money and handed it to Jacob. "Count it, Jonathon. I don't trust this nigga."

Jacob counted the money. It totaled three grand, the amount that Michael Riley told him he was to collect.

"It's all here."

Mario nodded. "Cool." He looked at Brick, then pointed his gun at the crook of his neck. "I outta smoke yo ass right here, bitch, for hiding from me so long. Tiring us out, chasing yo ass."

"Oh shit, Mario. Why don't you just chill?" Jacob insisted. "I need to get this to Mike. As long as we got the money that's all that matters."

"I-I wasn't . . . I—" Brick was stammering.

"You what? What you gotta say, nigga? Wha'?" Mario pressed the .38 harder into his neck.

"Damn!" Jacob exclaimed as he got out of the car.

He suddenly heard a puking sound, and then he smelled it in all its sour glory. He looked in the back of Mario's car to see Brick vomiting all over himself, Mario, and the seat.

"Oh fuck! I know you didn't!" Mario screamed. "Get the hell out my car! I oughta make you eat this shit!"

He pushed Brick out the door to the ground, then jumped out behind him, kicking him hard in the ribs. Brick cried out, jumped up, and took off.

"You see that shit?" Mario shouted again, looking at Jacob.

"Um . . . yeah. Kinda on the stank side."

Jacob was fighting hard not to laugh, but Mario's gansta ways got to him. He couldn't wait to bust his ass. He was one brotha that was deserving of everything that was coming to him.

"Listen, Mario. You'd better get outta here and get your car cleaned." He looked into the backseat again and put his fingers over his nose. "Maybe you should get it detailed." He laughed. "Aight, I'm out." Jacob made a phone gesture to his ear. "I'll call you."

Mario didn't hear him though. As Jacob was walking to his car he could still hear him cursing and complaining.

Jacob got in his Excursion and shook his head. His education in street life was making him very weary.

As he showered, Jacob thought about the situation with Mario and Brick. It had actually gone pretty good. Sometimes when he hooked up with Mario during collection time things would get violent. Brick was much older than the other guys Mario had running drugs for him. It was the kids, young brothas who didn't feel they had many options, other than selling drugs, who usually felt the heat of his anger. It was things like that that gave Jacob the fuel he needed to keep on his path. He didn't want to just get the little guys, or even the ones like Mario Lincoln, who led the small street army. He wanted the ones at the top. The problem was he wasn't completely sure who they all were yet, or rather he didn't have enough concrete proof.

He turned off the water that had started to get cold, stepped out of the shower, and looked in the mirror. He wiped the steam from the mirror.

"Not bad," Jacob stated as he turned his face left and right, examining himself at all angles. The neat, short beard that he had decided to grow when he took on this assignment gave his dark face character, lending him a rugged Othello look, he thought vainly. His eyes were dark and brooding, with long, fanlike lashes. He wore his black hair short, usually doing the do-rag thing each night to give him the waves that danced on the top. Women usually considered Jacob White attractive. What they didn't see was the man beneath the mask, and all the past hurt and devastation—the loss. He closed his eyes as the memories hit him again. He could see Regina's smooth, flawless, light brown skin; her tender brown eyes beckoning to him. His heart began to race; a feeling he got whenever he thought of his late wife, and the love they had shared since college. As he opened his eyes, it was his own reflection he saw, not Regina's. He sighed heavily.

The last time he had seen Regina and their beautiful princess,

Bali, felt just like yesterday. The morning kiss of good-bye that he and Regina always gave each other; that brush across the forehead he had given Bali, feeling the slight fever that baked her body. Something had told Jacob to stay home that day. That voice of God you sometimes hear, but usually ignore. But Bali was doing fine it seemed. He had already missed a couple of days at work. At the time he was working as a private investigator, and really working hard to make his business a success. He had no idea that that morning would be the last time he would see his family alive. He had no idea that the trip to the doctor's would end by an attempted carjacking and the shooting of his wife and three-year-old daughter.

Maybe if he had been with Regina. Maybe if he had taken his daughter to the doctor instead of being at work worrying about someone else's problems, it wouldn't have happened. But maybes didn't change reality. His tragedy changed him forever. He quit his job and mentally wandered for months until finally dusting himself off and deciding to join the Federal Bureau of Investigation. It would have been so much easier to just be a cop, but Jacob was a person who always felt it was better to get to the source of things. He wanted to get to the bone of the sickness in the society that bred criminals like the ones that killed his wife and daughter. And he needed to be more than a police officer to do that.

He worked undercover on many cases, first in D.C. and then L.A., and now finally ending up in New York. However, the other cases didn't get as close to what his original goal had been when he first joined the Bureau. For the past year he had a chance to get deep into the underworld of crime and corruption. But it seemed that the closer he got to getting all he needed on Michael Riley, the more corruption he found; more unbelievable characters that had their hands deep in the cookie jar.

Jacob did his nightly routine. He put a dab of Sportin' Waves pomade on his hair, brushed it, and then covered it with his do-rag. He slipped on a pair of gray cotton lounging pants, brushed his teeth, grabbed a beer, and then decided he would catch the featherweight boxing match that he heard would be on HBO that evening.

Once he had settled down to watch the fight, he heard a light tap at his front door.

"Damn," he exclaimed.

Whenever he tried to get a break there was always some type of interruption.

He walked to the door and looked out the peephole. Double damn, he thought. Lia. She was the last thing he needed to kill his groove. He opened the door.

"Hey, boo!" Lia exclaimed with a smile.

"What are you doing here, Lia?"

She brushed passed him, looking around at his place as if she was checking to see if he had other female company.

Lia was a Mackings dancer. One who felt she had dibs on Jacob for some odd reason. But then again, Lia thought she had dibs on every man who crossed her path.

Jacob leaned back against the door. "Why are you here, Lia?" he asked again.

"'Cause I missed you, Jon-Jon," she cooed.

"Jonathon."

"Jon-Jon to me . . ." She got up close to him, draping her arms around his neck. "You haven't been to any of the clubs lately. What's has you so busy, baby?"

Jacob laughed slightly. "I have more to do with my time than spending it watching you ladies shake it fast every single night." His eyebrows rose. "Aren't you dancing tonight?"

"Nope. I'm off, and we're on . . ." Lia rubbed her hands through his thick, curling chest hairs, all the way down to his muscular six-pack. Her long, painted fingertips scratched and flipped at the waist of his lounge pants before dipping farther. "I thought you would appreciate some feminine attention. See, aren't I sweet?" She winked.

Jacob cleared his throat. What could he say? He wasn't made of stone, that's for sure, and Lia wasn't a Plain Jane by any means. Her slanted green eyes, contacts of course, had seduction written all over them. He had seen her swivel and grind on the stage enough times to know what tasty treats she had to offer, and he had even given in to the temptations of the flesh a couple of times, grabbing a sample here and there. But tonight . . .

"Listen, baby, I want to chill tonight. My beer is getting hot and the fight is on." He pushed her away slightly. "Maybe . . ." Lia's eyes never left his. Then he felt her fingers slipping down farther, her nails scratching down the length of his hardening manhood. "Maybe we could do—" Jacob choked on his next words. He closed his eyes and moaned instead.

"Did you say something?" she purred. She laughed wickedly as she slid down in front of him to her knees. Jacob's pants came down next, and then Lia's hot touch.

Shit! Jacob thought a couple of hours later. He'd missed the fight. His dark body was encased in sweat, sweat that Lia was attempting to lick away as she ran her serpent tongue down the chiseled line of his abs.

"Come on, Lia, haven't you had enough?"

Lia laughed. "After only four orgasms? Nah. I'm betting on five, boo."

"No can do. I'm not a twenty-sumpin' brotha, you know. I hit thirty-two my last birthday."

"Well," she whispered as she slid up the length of his body, "you're in your prime then. I lubz a chocolate man who's mature and sexsational."

Jacob snickered. "And on that thought . . ." He flipped Lia over, landing her on her back beneath him. "You gotta go, shawty. I need to get some sleep."

"No-o-o-o," she protested. "Please, Jonathon. Let me stay the night."

"No can do," he said again. He got up and slipped on his robe, then handed Lia her clothes.

"Hmm . . . okay, what if I would tell you something that you will find *very* interesting? Would you let me stay then?"

"Interesting in what way?"

"Well . . ."

Jacob didn't know why, but Lia's irritating little "well . . . " that she always said was irking the crap outta him tonight. Straight up, he just wanted her to bounce. Maybe that was cold, seeing how he had just waxed that ass, but then again, who invited her over anyhow?

"Michael is opening four new clubs in Queens. Two of them he's having escorts, if you know what I mean," Lia finally said.

Jacob's eyebrows rose. "You mean the same way he has escorts at Mackings?"

"Who says he has escorts at Mackings?"

"Lia, please, I wasn't born yesterday. I know what's up, even if Michael does think I'm walking blind."

"Hmph! Well I bet you don't know how he's funding them."

"How?"

"You're gonna let me stay the night?"

"Ha!" He slapped Lia on the ass. "I can find out my own information. I really don't know how Mike is slipping to the point of letting you know so much anyhow. Besides, if he wants me to know how he's funding his operations he'll tell me himself."

"But you asked me about things like that once. I thought you were curious."

"I was just asking. Mike keeps me up on anything I need to know."

Jacob kept to himself the fact that he would be starting his seek and find first thing in the morning to learn more about Riley's new business ventures. He had to be getting the money from somewhere. Everything Michael Riley did was done on a huge scale. Jacob knew that he didn't have the capital at this time to purchase four new dance clubs throughout New York.

Lia still hadn't put her clothes back on. "You have to go, Lia. I told you, I want to get some sleep tonight."

"Pleeeeeeeease."

"Nope." He pushed her half-dressed body toward his bedroom door. "Out."

"You're a dog," she whined.

"And you're too horny."

The last thing he saw was her pout as he headed toward his bathroom to wash her scent off him.

3

New York City

Kimberla woke up with a yawn. By the time she reached Manhattan she was bushed. She figured it had more to do with the stress she'd dealt with while flying more than anything else. She reached for her bag, pulling out both her laptop and the folder she had swiped from Kyte Williams's office the day before. She could only imagine how much trouble she would be in once Kyte found out what she had done. At this point none of that mattered to her. She needed to know exactly where Margo had been working, how long, and what she had been doing. She flipped through the manila folder. It was very limited on information. The only thing that registered was that the agency sent Margo undercover to investigate information of a political nature. According to the file she was dancing at a club called Mackings. Now that Kimberla couldn't understand. What would Margo dancing at a club have to do with politics? The information in this file was pure garbage! Why was everything so secretive? Fiddling a bit more through the file, Kimberla noted the address and phone number. She may not know at the time what was going on, but she knew where to go to find out.

She grabbed the phone that sat on the end table by her bed. She quickly dialed the number to Mackings.

"Mackings!" a masculine voice sung out.

"Hello. I need to talk to someone about auditioning."

"Are you a dancer?"

At that question Kimberla knew that she would have to call in a favor from a friend of hers who worked in vital statistics. She needed to make sure that everything she told these Mackings people would come up true if they decided to do a background check on her.

"Yes I am. I've been dancing for years."

"So how old are you?" the guy asked. "We prefer younger women here, or rather our customers do."

Kimberla thought about that for a second. She knew she could easily pass for . . .

"I'm twenty-six. I started dancing when I was fourteen so I have plenty of experience, plus my body is tight and I look very young," she stated confidently.

The Mackings guy seemed to chew over that for a moment, before he finally came back with, "Okay. Why don't you come over around four? We're always looking for new girls, so if you have what it takes maybe we can use you. Wear something sexy and be ready to take it all off, all right?"

Take it all off. Kimberla had to pause on that one. But she would do whatever she had to do to get to the bottom of things. She wondered if Margo had been *taking it all off* when she was dancing at Mackings.

"I'll be there."

She was about to hang up when he asked, "What's your name?"

"Alisha Howard," Kimberla replied.

"Okay, Alisha, I'm Michael Riley, the owner of Mackings and most of the adult establishments in this area in case you didn't know. I'll see you at four."

He then hung up the phone.

The owner of most of the adult establishments in the area.

Interesting, Kimberla thought. She was looking forward to meeting Michael Riley.

Kimberla knew she couldn't go to her audition without being hooked up to the nine. When she used to work undercover years ago she had become known for her unique ability to transform herself in her many *skins*; thus the pet nickname given to her, Chameleon. She hadn't had a reason to test her acting ability and change her skin since she had become a SAIC, but just like you never forgot how to ride a bike, a true Chameleon never forgot the trick of masking it.

She stepped into Macy's an hour later, went into the woman's department, and smiled sweetly at the saleswoman who eyed her like she was her next check.

"Can I help you?" the woman asked.

Kimberla looked over the array of fancy dance outfits that filled the racks of eveningwear. "I'm a dancer. I'm looking for a few outfits that loosen easily. But not too easily."

"Oh!" The saleswoman's eyes got wide. "You mean like exotic dancing?"

Kimberla laughed slightly. "Um . . . yeah."

"Whoa! Okay," the saleswoman stammered, "I'm sure I have something you'll be interested in."

They walked around a bit, fiddling through the rows of clothing. Most of it was a bit too outlandish and flashy for Kimberla's taste. She wasn't sure how she would feel about nude dancing, but she knew she had to wear something revealing, and was very thankful she had stuck to her workout sessions throughout the years. The fact that she had a second-degree belt in Kajukenbo and was a Taebo enthusiast didn't hurt either. She knew how to work her body when necessary.

Twenty minutes later she caught sight of the perfect dance outfit. Maybe some wouldn't really call it an outfit, but that's all it was to her. Everything Kimberla did, she did with style. Even if it was exotic dancing, she thought.

It was a knee-length, soft, burgundy, chiffon wrap, which

she knew would cling sensuously to her bare skin. She chose a pink thong to wear under it.

She looked in the mirror facing her in the changing room. Even with her darker-hued complexion she almost saw a blush rise in her cheeks at the thought of men watching her shake her booty, coochie outline and all, visible to their sex-greedy eyes.

After having made her purchase at Macy's, Kimberla went down a few blocks farther to Lira's Hair and Nails. She had let her hair grow out for the past year, but was now about to do what she had been craving for a while, cut it all off. Two hours later she was set. She looked in the mirror. Left, right, and to the side. Her hair that once was to her jawline now laid flat but swinging at the tips of her ears. Dyed a dark burgundy and wrapped, she was looking pretty hot. She grabbed her bags, and hailed a taxi.

By 3:15 Kimberla was dressed and ready. She decided to dress down for her interview, so that she would shine during her dance performance. Her eyes were already sparkling as her cab road the Manhattan Bridge, heading to Brooklyn. In order to change her look, she donned hazel contacts that set her new hairdo off perfectly.

The yellow cab pulled up to a club spot. One of the buildings had Mackings written in fancy fonts and a high-heeled shoe dangling off the "S" at the end. This was her destination.

"Thanks," she said to the cabby, handing him a twenty. "Keep the change."

Kimberla was pretty impressed with the stylish look of the place. She took a deep breath before waltzing inside. She smiled at the heavyset guard that stood statuesquely at the entranceway.

"I have an appointment with Michael Riley," she told the security guard.

He looked her up and down, suspiciously.

"Oh yeah? What are you? Another stripper?"

"I'm a *dancer,*" Kimberla said, correcting him. Smug mo-ther-fuck-er is he, she thought.

"Yeah, right." He smirked. "So whas' ya name, Miss Dancer?"

"Alisha, Alisha Howard. And he *is* expecting me."

The guard smiled at her again.

"Follow me."

He then swung his big hand toward a double set of doors that was a few feet down an empty hallway. "You're walking too slow," he said.

"Good grief," Kimberla hissed to herself.

The guy seemed to hear her whispering. He turned around and grinned as he opened the double doors. Kimberla decided to ignore him, and instead focused on the tall, distinguished brotha that stood at a wet bar fixing a drink.

"Hey, boss, you have an appointment with this lady?"

The guy, who Kimberla assumed to be Michael Riley, turned around and nodded. "Thanks, Jones." He looked at Kimberla. "You're Alisha Howard?"

"Yes, I am," she said. She walked quickly toward him and extended her hand. "It's very nice to meet you, Mr. Riley."

"Call me Mike." He shook her hand with a firm grip.

"Call me Alisha," Kimberla shot back sweetly.

Sizing Michael Riley up, Kimberla decided that he was quite good looking. About 6'1", medium, buff build, dark brooding eyes, and light brown complexion. He had the curly hair thing going on that was very well groomed. Even though he owned and ran a dance/strip joint, he was styling in one of those expensive Armani suits as if he were Donald Trump himself.

Kimberla could tell that he was also sizing her up. But she knew she didn't have to worry. A woman knows when she is looking good. And with all the money she had spent getting a look that cried dancer, he'd better be taking careful note.

"Nice," Michael finally said. He looked again at the security guard that he had called Jones. "Get lost," he told him.

Giving her a slow up and down look of appreciation, Jones winked, then made his way out the door.

"Have a seat," Michael said after the door shut. Kimberla did so.

"So, what made you look us up here at Mackings? Tell me a bit about yourself."

Kimberla took a deep breath. "Well, I've been dancing for twelve years—"

"Where are you from?" he broke in.

"Maryland." She thought back to the information she had fed Jerry, her statistics friend. "I studied at Junipers School of Dance since I was fourteen."

Michael laughed slightly. "Well it sounds like you were taught a different type of dancing from what my ladies do here, Alisha."

"Yes, true. But I can adjust to just about anything."

"Do you have a problem with showing that delectable body of yours?"

Kimberla swallowed hard. "No. Not really. But we are talking about topless, right? I noticed that you advertise for topless and full nudity. I was thinking more on the line of topless."

"Hmm . . ." Michael hummed. He then looked down to her breasts. "Stand up for me."

Standing up slowly, Kimberla held her body at a model stance. Her breasts were round and shapely, size thirty-four C, her waistline a small, tight twenty-three inches. Her hips were not really curvy and only measured a slim thirty-four. But her legs were her saving grace. Long, sexy, Tina Turner legs. Her boo-friend, Brandon, was always telling her that she needed to have those babies insured.

She flexed her shapely calves as Michael continued his observation. At moments like this she was glad that God had blessed her with good parents and good genes.

"Not bad," he finally said. "Are you prepared to show me what you can do on stage?"

"Sure am," Kimberla said with confidence.

She followed Michael Riley. Her heart was beating rapidly as he led her out of his office.

The sounds of singer Kelis's "Milkshake" filled the room. Kimberla would have chosen a calmer song to dance to, but she figured Michael wanted to see if her milkshake could bring all the boys to his club, she thought with a laugh.

Her medium-brown skin was coated with a thin layer of glitter; her eyes shined, and her freshly cut hair, even in its shortness, bobbed and swung around her head in a sexy toss as she put her all into her performance. She swiveled with her eyes closed, trying hard to remember the dance moves that her instructor had taught her years back. (She actually had taken dance classes back in the day.)

Once the inspiration hit her, she decided to also incorporate her training in Kajukenbo, which was a mixture of dance and martial arts. Her long legs were taut and strong as she kicked them out, pointing her toes. She then slowed down and gripped her naked breast, bringing her mouth down to her nipple; she flicked her tongue at it rapidly like a cobra. That caught Michael Riley's attention. Desire coated his eyes as she pranced her thong-clad womanhood in his face. Kimberla almost laughed at his heated expression. Men were such silly puppy dogs, she thought. Amazingly, instead of the dance embarrassing her, she felt almost powerful. If she wasn't such a die-hard FBI agent, she would consider a career move. She snickered inside at the thought of that.

As the music came to an end she continued to stand in front of him, breathing hard as she waited for him to speak. He was quiet for a moment, just staring at her. Finally he spoke.

"Very nice. Very different. *Very* sexy."

He came up on the stage, circling around Kimberla slowly.

"You're not what we normally have around here—not necessarily a drop-dead beauty. But you are sexy . . . and exotic."

No, this hen-pecked bastard did not just tell me that I am not a beauty! Kimberla thought heatedly.

"I think our gentlemen audience will love you. So will the ladies. When can you start?"

"When do you want me to start?"

"How about tomorrow night?"

"That's fine with me." She smirked.

"Okay," he said, clasping his hands together. "We need a stage name for you. Do you want to be introduced as Alisha? I think you need something a bit more exotic, like you."

"Well, perhaps something like . . . Chameleon?" Kimberla suggested. She smiled at her own audacity.

"Chameleon. The skin-changing reptile. That fits you," Michael said. "Chameleon it is."

Kimberla and Michael looked up at the sound of footsteps coming toward the dance stage. A tall, dark-skinned man, dressed in black jeans, a white-and-black Fubu T-shirt, and a black Berretta cap walked toward them.

"Jonathon!" Michael exclaimed. "I've been waiting all day for you, brother!"

Kimberla froze instantly. She didn't even notice that her burgundy wrap was flying open, showing all the goods that she had just advertised to Michael Riley.

Michael jumped off the stage. "I want you to meet our next Mackings sensation." He put his hand out to Kimberla, taking hold of hers. She walked forward, slowly.

"This is Chameleon. She's gonna burn this stage up tomorrow night, right, sister?" He winked at her.

Kimberla couldn't answer him. She was too busy looking into the familiar, dark brown eyes of Special Agent Jacob White.

4

New York City

Ever since he had been a freshman in college Jacob knew he needed glasses. He always put that off, figuring that his eyes were his best features. So he wanted to keep them all out and visible. He never did get an examination. But as he stood in front of the woman he knew to be Special Agent in Charge Kimberla Bacon from Washington, D.C., he figured this was God's way of telling him to get a second pair of eyes, and fast!

Kimberla's mouth opened and closed like a water-starved fish, and she was speechless as Michael Riley said, "Jon, this is Alisha Howard. Alisha, Jonathon Simmons. He works for one of my other establishments."

Kimberla eyes grew huge as Jacob White reached his hand out to her. Clear recognition shined in her eyes. Shock, heat, and surprise were in his as he looked down at her breasts that were still visible and bare.

"It's nice meeting you, Jonathon," she said, as she closed her wrap tightly around her.

"Likewise," he said. What was she doing here? he thought. His eyes wandered back to her breasts.

"What do you think?" Michael Riley asked him.

"Nice," Jacob stated with his eyes glued to Kimberla's.

"I'd better go change," she said uncomfortably.

As she walked away Michael and Jacob looked at each other. Michael gave a low whistle. "Nice huh? Okay, come on to my office."

Jacob gave a parting glance to the swaying backside of Kimberla before following Michael to his office. Once they were inside, Michael set at his desk chair and faced Jacob.

"So, how do you think things are going with Mario?"

Jacob paused for a moment before he spoke. His mind was still doing a spin over having seen Kimberla. He hoped the Bureau wasn't about to make the same mistake they had made with Margo Hunter.

"Where's your mind, brother?" Michael asked, fanning his hand in front of Jacob's face.

"Oh! It's going well. Although Mario is a hothead. He's dangerous, Mike."

"Mario has always been a hothead. Dangerous? Nah, only in his own mind." Michael opened a gold container on his desk that was filled with white, imported peppermints. He pushed the container toward Jacob, offering him one. Jacob shook his head. "Anyhow, it's one of the reasons I wanted you to work with him. You're a levelheaded brotha, Jon. With Mario's street sense, he can go far. With your common sense and brains, you can go further, and keep trigger-happy fools like him in line."

"You think so?" Jacob said, laughing.

"I *know* so. Anyhow, the real deal starts now." He pushed a leather folder at Jacob. "Check that out," he said.

Jacob leafed through papers that were done up as a legitimate proposal, but it really was plans for the illegal transporting of drugs. It included a shipment from Saudi Arabia.

"Saudi Arabia?"

Michael grinned mischievously. "No one would ever suspect, would they?"

"I don't get it." Jacob shook his head.

"That's exactly the point. No one would ever suspect that our product would be coming from there."

"But still, how would you get it in without customs finding it? The crackdown is heavy. Especially since nine-eleven," Jacob pointed out.

"That's not our only pickup spot, Jon. And the thing is we've already started the operation. We've been at it a long-ass time. Believe me we are getting through with no problem. And not just from the Middle East. How do you think our family has been lucky enough to keep up the quality of product we have without it costing us an arm and a leg the way it does everyone else?"

"How?"

Before Michael could answer, his phone rang. "Mike here," he said. "Hello, how are you? Hold up." He looked at Jacob. "Listen, this is an important call. Can you wait outside just for a minute?"

"Sure thing," Jacob said.

He got up and walked outside of the office, feeling rather antsy at the interruption. For sure he needed to know more about this operation that Michael had going on. It could be the key to finally finding out who his political contacts were. If that could be found out, and if Jacob could finally pin not only Michael Riley but all the dirty higher-ups who supported his drug trade, maybe Jacob could go home. That is, wherever home would be for him once he was no longer undercover and could start living a normal life again. He was getting very weary of New York, Mackings, and especially Michael Riley.

Ten minutes later he was still tapping his foot impatiently as he waited outside of Michael's office. Riley had a bad habit of expecting everyone to beckon to any and everything he wanted. But Michael wasn't who filled his mind at the moment. The image of Kimberla Bacon, her round behind and full breasts flying on the stage, was unforgettable. What the hell was she doing in New York? he thought to himself.

After she went backstage to change clothes, Jacob had to shake off the shock and fix a normal look on his face. But he still couldn't get her out of his mind.

Five minutes later Kimberla walked down the hallway toward him. She carefully avoided his eyes, looking in every direction but his.

"Kim—" he started.

Kimberla put her hand up and shook her head rapidly. "It's Alisha," she whispered. She got up closer to Jacob. "What are you doing here?"

"Me?" Jacob asked in astonishment. "What are *you* doing here? That should be the question."

Before she could answer, Michael Riley opened the door to his office.

"Sorry about that, Jon." He looked at Kimberla. "Good job, Alisha. I'll see you tomorrow night, okay? Be here at nine-thirty."

"I will!" Kimberla said quickly. She looked toward Jacob, swallowed hard, and started walking toward the main door.

Jacob addressed Michael. "Listen, I need to roll out, but I'm gonna get back at you with what we talked about, okay?" He started walking quickly to catch up with Kimberla.

"What's the hurry, brother?" Michael called out. He snickered knowingly to himself. "Go get her, man!"

Jacob looked back at him and laughed. "I have an appointment, that's it. Besides, you kept me waiting too long." He disappeared out the door behind Kimberla.

She was standing at the curb trying to hail a taxi when Jacob tapped her on the shoulder. She turned around to him.

"Our ride is that way," he said, pointing toward his Ford Excursion.

"I'm fine. It doesn't take long for a taxi in Brooklyn."

Jacob gave her a hard look. "Don't game with me, okay?"

He put his hand under her elbow and guided her in his direction. Once they were at his vehicle, he disarmed the alarm and then opened the passenger door. Oddly enough Kimberla didn't seem to have much fight in her. Which was just as well, Jacob thought. She had a hell of a lot of explaining to do. Either she or someone from the Feds needed to do some fast talking.

He slipped in the driver's seat, put his key in the ignition, then looked at her.

"Well?"

"Well what?" she asked.

"What's going on here? What are you doing in New York?"
Kimberla's eyes widen. "Shouldn't that be obvious?"

"No." Jacob laughed without mirth. "What's obvious is that
you Feds are running a damn game without telling me what's
up. And I don't like that shit *at all . . .*"

"No one is running a game on you, Jacob. And why are you
saying us Feds? What are you?"

Jacob was getting a bit tired of the word games. It irritated
him how the Bureau had slipped Kimberla Bacon in on him
without letting him know. They were definitely getting sloppy.
Surprise was something that Michael Riley could easily read on
a person's face. Fortunately, he had taken Kimberla Bacon's
surprised expression to mean that she was attracted to Jacob.
That thought gave him pause. Her shock was indeed evident.
The question was, why?

"Didn't you know I've been working on Michael Riley's case
for the past year?" he asked her.

"No, I didn't."

"Is that why you looked so surprised when you saw me?"

Jacob could tell that Kimberla was uncomfortable. That was
not the norm for her. He had known her for years, even before
he joined the Federal Bureau of Investigation, and one word
was always a staple adjective for Kimberla Bacon: self-assured.

Jacob gave her a hard stare. Something wasn't quite right.
"Tell me something," he said, "when did you start doing undercover work again, Ms. Special Agent in Charge Bacon?"

Kimberla caught her breath as Jacob suddenly slammed on
the brakes, barely missing a ragged stray dog that limped piti-
fully across the busy street.

"Damn!" Jacob exclaimed. He pulled over to the side of the
road.

Kimberla waited a second before she spoke. "Do you always
drive so recklessly?"

"Let's not change the subject. I wanna know what's going
on. I think, seeing that I'm working and risking my life with

cats like Riley, the least thing the Bureau could do is warn me when anything is changed or when they are sending an agent to work around me."

"Well . . ." Kimberla paused.

"Well what?"

"No one knows I'm here. I'm actually away on vacation and that is all they know." Her words came out in a rush. Jacob could tell that she was holding her breath, waiting for his response.

Not being able to hold it in, he burst out laughing.

"What's so funny?" Kimberla demanded. Her eyes were smarting.

"Kimberla Bacon. I can't believe you of all people are breaking the rules!"

"I'm not—" she started.

"Why would you be working undercover without . . . who? Kyte Williams is head investigator in your division now, right? He doesn't know you're here? What are you after?"

"I want to know what happened to Margo Hunter."

Bingo, Jacob thought. Kimberla probed his face thoughtfully.

"You did know she was working for Michael Riley, right? You two knew about each other?" she asked.

"I recognized Margo, just like I recognized you." His eyebrow rose. "And I'm telling you the same thing I told her. This is no place for you."

"Wait a minute!" Kimberla sat forward. "Do you realize that she's missing?"

"Of course I do. The DEA keeps tabs on things, too, you know."

This time Kimberla's voice was at a screaming pitch. "If you knew about her and if you know that she's missing then you should understand why I'm here!"

"So you figured you would just come without authorization and do your own thing and that no one would find out about it?" Jacob asked.

Kimberla gave Jacob an innocent look. "I'm just dancing. I

just wanted to get a feel for what Margo was doing here, that's all."

"Right," Jacob huffed. He shifted his gears back from park to drive. "So now that you know it shouldn't be a problem with you taking your ass back to D.C. ASAP."

"Wait. Help me, Jacob. Please . . ." she whispered.

"Help you what?"

"Help me to find out what happened to her—to Margo. What do you know? Where was she staying? When was the last time you saw her?"

"I only talked with her one time." Jacob was evasive.

"And what happened?" Kimberla pressed.

"That was when I told her that the Bureau should never have put her on this case. A week later I got word that she had disappeared, and I never heard from her or saw her again."

Kimberla nodded her head. "Okay." She swallowed hard and closed her eyes as she leaned her head back against the seat.

"Look, Kimberla . . . Agent Bacon, it's not like I don't care what happened to Margo Hunter. I do. It's just that it's not up to me to find that out. It's not up to you either. Especially if you weren't assigned to this case. I need to get you to your hotel so that you can pack and get the first flight out."

"I will not!"

"You will too!"

Both of them looked at each other with stormy eyes. Kimberla's suddenly softened, taking on a pleading look.

"Listen, I know the agency is looking into this, but Margo was my friend. I'm not hurting anyone by checking on things, am I? I can't just sit around and do nothing," she explained. "Jacob, I could *really* use your help."

Jacob's eyes widened. "And bust my cover? Hell no! Let the Bureau do their job. Neither you nor I need to be in this."

"I *am* the Bureau, and so are you. Why can't we work together? You are close enough to Michael Riley to get far more info than anyone else. And now that I'm a Mackings dancer—"

"That's another thing," he cut in. "What possessed you to

think you could get into Mackings and strut your stuff without being in a hell of a lot of trouble when Kyte Williams finds out?"

Jacob almost laughed at Kimberla's surprised look.

"See, I know that he is still running things in D.C., and I also know that he'll have your head on a platter when he finds out you're up here."

"Then we'll just have to make sure he doesn't," Kimberla said smugly.

"We?"

"Yes." She smiled. "Being the wonderful, supportive, former college buddy that you are, I know you'll keep this quiet for me, right?"

"Wrong." Jacob snickered.

"Jacob, please . . ."

Jacob's eyes meshed with Kimberla's. For some odd reason he felt an uncomfortable hardness growing in his jeans. She looked hot on that stage. He could still picture her brown skin with its sparkling glow—those breasts. The throb in his jeans grew to an ache. If she could move him as she did, surely she could pull off a masquerade for Riley, he reasoned. He just couldn't and wouldn't let her in on his cover. He had worked too hard to get it, and he wanted Riley and his political allies too badly to fuck up now.

"Jacob?" Kimberla said, shaking him from his thoughts.

"How do you plan to do this? How long do you plan to stay?"

"I just want to know what happened to her. After that it's all yours. I'm not trying to get involved in your business."

"So once you find out, you will leave, right?"

"Scout's honor," Kimberla said, crossing her fingers.

"Okay. I'll be quiet. For now," he said with emphasis. Kimberla started smiling before Jacob cut her off with, "But don't get in my way, Kimberla. And once I say it's time for you to leave I don't want you trying to pull fuckin' rank. Or I'll pull rank and call Kyte Wiliams. I don't want you to do anything that I don't know about first. Is that understood?"

"Totally," Kimberla agreed, smiling. "We're a team now."

"Hmm . . ." Jacob hummed. "I hope I won't regret this."

Whether she was a chameleon or not, her skins better be airtight with this one. Everything he had worked for was riding on it.

Everything.

5

New York City

Jacob White. It had been so long since she had seen that man.

As the hot water washed over Kimberla's skin, she relived the embarrassment she felt when she saw and recognized him at Mackings. She was sure that her job and her chance to help Margo were busted. But now instead of a possible snitch, she had a co-spy.

She stepped out of the shower and grabbed the plush towel hanging on the rack. Looking in the mirror, she pulled off the shower cap that protected her newly cut hairdo. She looked good. And obviously Michael Riley thought so, too, since he didn't hesitate to hire her right after the audition.

Her mind wandered back to Jacob. She had promised him she would leave as soon as she found out what happened to Margo. That was a laugh. Didn't he know her better than that? She would stay as long as she had to stay, even if it did mean working with someone who thought they were in control of things.

Pure madness. It was a shame to lose a good agent to the likes of the DEA. She had heard he was now working undercover for them. But it had been a long time since she had seen or heard from him.

She remembered years ago, when they were both at Georgetown U. He was then and still was now just as handsome as he could be. Her infatuation with him had no limits back then. But he hadn't known it existed. He was too much into his college love, Regina Watson. That was all cool, but he was Kimberla's first and only major crush. When she heard that Regina was pregnant and that Jacob was going to marry her, Kimberla had been heartbroken. Since then, she saved the heartbreak bullshit for sissy women, and focused on her career. However, seeing him had brought it all back for her, almost. She still didn't have time to let her emotions get tangled into the crafty web women fall into. Jacob was single now. She had been so jealous of Regina Watson, but was horrified when she heard about her murder and the murder of their daughter. Never having really talked with him about it, she had no doubt of his devastation and despair. But life was like that. Full of heartache and tears when you allowed love to flow within it. She never wanted to put herself out there and feel anything close to the kind of pain love can bring. Not that she had ever been hurt by a man. But she had seen and heard enough from her girlfriends. And even had felt the inner embarrassment of her secret crush on Jacob, knowing he would never want her anyhow. She knew the words to that song, "Love Don't Live Here Anymore," but for her it never had.

The time since she had auditioned had passed by fast, and it was now time for her to live up to Michael Riley's expectations. It was 7:45 the following evening. Dressed in her best nighttime party gear—a black, thigh-length jersey knit and black stiletto pumps—Kimberla smirked. She knew she was looking good. She shook her head at her vanity. She had to get to Mackings in time. She didn't have time to primp, or think about her past lack of loves, or whatever one would call it.

Tonight she had chosen the snake outfit that she had purchased during her short shopping spree and hair and eye makeover. It was a long brown and black, see-through nightie.

Underneath she would wear a black thong. She also picked her own music. This was her dance, her thing, her music. Whether or not Michael Riley would let her do her thing remained to be seen. She laughed a bit to herself. She was really getting into this dance thing. But her real goal was right in front of her.

Kimberla was getting more and more concerned about Margo. The longer she was missing the more chances were that she was probably dead. The thought of that caused cold chills to run up the course of her spine, and it weakened her. There were few people who had made an impact on her life the way Margo had. What was so odd was that even though Margo was white, she was more like one of Kimberla's sista girls. Every step she had made, Margo had been right there beside her. She knew Margo's parents—had spent time with them at family cookouts and gatherings—and Margo had spent time with Kimberla's father and stepmother. She had been there holding Kimberla's hand when her father got married, helping her deal with the inner conflict of seeing her dad with someone else. They had that kind of friendship. So Kimberla felt she owed it to her friend to do more than just worry about her. She had to find her. Or at least find out what happened to her so that she could give Margo's family some sense of peace.

Kimberla felt moisture gathering. She sniffed, putting a finger at each corner of her eyes to stop the tears that were threatening to trickle down her cheeks.

"Damn it!" she said out loud to herself. "I will not let myself get like this. Kimberla Bacon does not cry!" She looked in the mirror one last time. "Time to get to work, girl."

Grabbing her small, vinyl suitcase and black bag, she made her way out of her hotel room to hail a cab.

At night, Mackings had a totally different aura than it did when Kimberla auditioned the day before. The nighttime crowd was massive. She stepped out of the cab. Her long legs were accentuated by four-inch pumps. She paid the cab driver his fee and made her way inside. As she walked past the crowd of wannabe customers, vying to get through the doors of Mackings, she spotted Jones, the security guard she had met the evening before who had gotten cute with her. He smiled at her as she met his eye.

"Hello there," he said, eying her up and down.

Kimberla nodded to him and made her way inside the club. "Is Michael Riley here?"

"Yup, but he's busy in the back."

"So where should I go?" Kimberla asked.

Jones laughed. "In the back."

He was being sarcastic of course. It wasn't taking Kimberla long to see that this Jones was a big-headed wiseass. She smiled at him as she made her way down the noisy, crowded hallway. As she disappeared behind the hard wooden doors that led to the backstage dressing room, she breathed a sigh of relief. At least she had made it this far. She glanced at two other dancers who looked at her curiously.

"Hey there," one of the girls said, smiling brightly. "Are you new?"

"Yes. My first night," Kimberla said in a breathless voice.

The girl who had spoken walked up to her, holding her hand out.

"I'm Delphi." She looked toward the door as her partner girlfriend looked Kimberla up and down, then went inside the dressing room. Delphi shook her head and laughed. "Don't pay her any mind. That's Lia Chamberlayne. She's a rude bitch. What's your name?"

"Alisha Howard."

Delphi was a cute sista, kind of short. But then any woman would be short compared to Kimberla's tallness. Delphi had a light brown complexion with matching light brown hair that met her shoulders in a straight swinging bob. She looked a bit sweaty as if she had just finished her performance.

"Come on inside," she said to Kimberla.

Kimberla followed her. The noisiness of the dressing room greeted them. Wall-to-wall women were there that were naked, half naked, or wearing outfits so skimpy and revealing that they may as well have been naked.

"Hey, you gutter-trash hoes, this is Alisha!" Delphi shouted.

The other dancers responded with smiles and hellos. All except for Lia, who instead of looking in her direction was busy removing her makeup.

Just as Delphi was finishing introductions, the dressing room door opened, and in walked Michael Riley. He smiled at Kimberla when he saw her.

"Well hello, Miss Chameleon."

"Hello, Michael," Kimberla said sweetly.

"So, you are ready to set it off tonight?"

Kimberla looked at Delphi, whose eyebrows rose up and down in a comical fashion. She could also feel Lia Chamberlayne's eyes beaming into her back.

"I'm ready." She breathed.

Michael gave her bottom a quick squeeze.

"Okay, get changed. You're on in an hour."

The roar of the audience was deafening. Obviously the men and some women were enjoying the show, and screaming for more. Kimberla felt tense and nervous as she stood at the partitions separating the stage from the dressing room area. Delphi had gone out for her second dance and was just finishing up. As her music ended she breezed past Kimberla, signaling thumbs up. Delphi's encouragement didn't do much to dissolve the knot that was growing bigger and bigger in Kimberla's stomach. The butterflies intensified even more when the announcer started introducing her.

"We have some fresh new beauty and talent for you all tonight. She is truly a chocolate delight. The epitome of sensual sin, sent from above just to please you men! Gentlemen, ladies, we present to you, Chameleon!"

The sounds of Truth Hurts crooned from the speakers. The seductive words of the song, "Addictive," had Kimberla swiveling onto the stage. She fixed a sensual smile on her face. She was aiming to please not the crowd, but Michael Riley, who watched her with half-closed eyes from a corner front row table. The audience seemed to be captivated by Kimberla's unique dance style as she slowly unveiled herself. She eased herself toward Michael's table, and at once spotted Jacob White. He glanced at her, frowning slightly, then looked directly at her nipples. They hardened instantly. For some reason knowing that Jacob was watching gave Kimberla the energy she needed to finish her dance.

She got to her knees, then flattened herself to the floor and slithered on her stomach like a snake toward Jacob's table. Propping herself on the edge of the stage, she focused solely on him. Her long nails scratched around her belly button; moved up her torso to the sculptured line leading to her cleavage. Kimberla's eyes met Jacob's. She didn't blink. Her nails then went to either breast, rolling her dark nipples around . . . around . . .

Pop! Pop! Pop!

Shocked out of her trance, Kimberla immediately jumped off of the stage. She reached instinctively at her hip for her pistol then remembered she was barely covered.

"What the hell was that?" she heard Jacob say.

Michael Riley had gone quickly to the floor also, trying to shield himself.

The crowd went wild, running in each direction to get away from what they thought were gunshots. After a moment of delirium, the DJ's voice came over the loud speaker.

"Sorry, people, a speaker went out. No need to panic. Everybody just calm down."

The DJ seemed to be almost laughing. Kimberla didn't see anything funny about it, especially not during her debut dance. She stood up abruptly.

"You need to get yourself covered," she suddenly heard Jacob say from close behind her. He handed her the snake-skinned, see-through robe she had come on stage with and then draped it around her shoulders. Kimberla slipped her arms in the holes.

"Thanks," she whispered.

She wasn't sure what this thing was that was developing between Jacob and her. Perhaps it was the atmosphere of the club, or the fact that she was half naked. But either way there was definitely some hot chemistry going on; at least on her part.

Michael Riley had disappeared, probably to curse out the DJ. Over half the audience had left, which would cut into drink sales tremendously. With a fifteen-dollar cover charge and ten-dollar drink minimum, he really didn't have much reason to complain though. But Kimberla guessed that a man like Michael Riley always cared when it came to dollars and cents; otherwise he wouldn't be doing any and everything he could to make new ones.

Kimberla turned to make her way backstage. She suddenly felt as naked as she was, and wanted to quickly put her debut to an end. She took three steps before she felt Jacob's hand touching her upper arm. She paused.

"Meet me in the lobby in an hour, okay?"

"Why?" Kimberla asked, looking into his eyes.

"Just be there," Jacob pressed.

Nodding in agreement, Kimberla wondered what Jacob wanted to talk to her about. She made her way back to the dressing room just as the announcer began apologizing to the audience for the chaotic interruption. Smiling to herself, Kimberla thought it was more than chaotic. In a place like Brooklyn a shoot-out in a nightclub was something to beware of, definitely.

An hour later Kimberla was dressed in her black jersey evening dress and waiting patiently for Jacob at the lobby entrance. She had thought Michael would want to talk to her about her dance performance, which was cut off, but with the problem that had occurred earlier he had disappeared for the evening. Kimberla looked down at her watch, checking the time. She had been waiting for Jacob for ten minutes now, and was getting a bit annoyed. She suddenly heard the sound of hand clapping behind her.

"Bravo! Bravo!" Jacob exclaimed, smiling as he walked up behind her. "You were doing a marvelous job just now."

"Why, thank you."

Jacob leaned closed, whispering for her ears only. "I wonder what Kyte would say if he could have seen you sliding across that floor, Agent Bacon?"

"You're trying to be funny, huh?"

Jacob laughed. "I'm just giving you a hard time."

"What did you want to see me for, smarty pants?"

"Well." A serious look suddenly coated Jacob's face. He looked around them cautiously before continuing. "I heard from FBI headquarters in D.C."

"What do you mean you heard from them? You didn't say anything about me, did you?"

"No, of course not. But they did ask a lot of questions about Margo Hunter. They wanted to know how much I knew about Michael's operations in his dance clubs and when was the last time I had seen her. You see, I'm investigating his drug connections. Like I told you before, I didn't have any contact with Margo."

"So what did you tell them?"

Jacob shrugged. "I told them exactly what I'm telling you. You may be banging your head up against an iron wall here."

"I'll decide that for myself," Kimberla whispered.

"So in the meantime you're gonna keep shaking your ass for Michael?"

"You seemed to be enjoying it." Kimberla smirked.

Jacob had the audacity to blush. He turned his head slightly toward the exiting doors, not looking at her as he said, "Anyhow, I just wanted to let you know to keep your eyes open. With them going so far as to contact me, that says that an investigation may be starting soon of her whereabouts. That means you might want to rethink what you're doing here, Kimberla."

Kimberla's heart started beating fast. She knew Jacob was right. How much time did she really have before Kyte sent someone to New York to start snooping around? And who would he send? Malcolm Johnson most likely. He would definitely be a thorn in her spine. Things had to move just a little bit faster. She would just have to start working on Delphi ASAP. Get her number, get her trust, and find out what she knew about Margo. With her mind focusing on that plan, Kimberla was shocked when all of a sudden Jacob pulled her roughly to him, covering her mouth with his. Surprise is what made her open her mouth, she told herself as his tongue invaded her. Surprise is what made her moan slightly at the tingles that started at her toes and worked their way up to dance in her tummy. She found herself kissing him back with equal enthusiasm. And almost forgot who she was until she heard a deep, amused voice behind her.

"I see I was right about you two."

Turning around quickly, Kimberla felt her embarrassment surfacing at the big grin on Michael Riley's face.

"Right about what?" Jacob asked.

Michael put his arm casually around Kimberla, who still had not voiced a word. "The vibe, brother. Yeah, I knew you had the hots for our Chameleon here. And that's okay." He squeezed her shoulder, laughing. "I just need you to come finish your dance set. We need to get our audience happy again. At least the ones who decided to stay."

Kimberla was quiet, not quite knowing what to say, especially feeling embarrassed as she did getting caught by Michael. Doing . . . *what the hell was Jacob doing?*

"So I'll call you later, okay?" Jacob said to her.

Giving him a tight smile, Kimberla nodded her response. She would definitely be talking to him later. She brushed past Michael Riley, as he said in a soft voice, "Break a leg, Chameleon."

6

New York City

The crowd cheered at their favorite political candidates. Goaded on by egos and hopes of a positive response, all the politicians' smiles were wide and beaming. Senator David Huggins was among the distinguished group. A short man with a strong, slim build, he was repped to be a sure bet to win the nomination for the Democratic bid for governor. As he was introduced to the audience, he moved with a sure, steady gait. He was welcomed with joyful enthusiasm.

"Thank you, ladies and gentlemen, my fellow senators, and congressmen. Mayor Judith Miller and distinguished representatives from the Democratic caucus, I thank you all. I don't need to introduce myself because you all know me. You all know what I stand for. You know what I will do for New York because you have worked with me or have aided me in my endeavors as senator. I come to you today to ask for further aid. The state of New York is in a dire situation. Drugs and gangs have infiltrated our streets, poisoning our children and teenagers. Crack babies and HIV-positive newborns are becoming an epidemic. Who will be their savior? And how can you save them?

How can you, as citizens of the great state of New York, the city of dreams, the melting pot, save our children from this devastation?"

The audience listened intently at Senator Huggins's powerful words, seemingly captivated by what he always did best. Huggins had always been able to win over a crowd. From his high school days as senior class president, his college days at NYU, staged rallies, and working as a lobbyist, David Huggins had always been the perfect speaker and politician.

His eyes widened as he continued to speak.

"Drugs are not the only demons on our streets. What about the weapons that control the masses? How many times have we heard about a young girl or boy gunned down in their own home by gangbangers and street thugs? The guns are usually sold on the streets by illegal smugglers and lowlifes. It's time for us to take back control of our neighborhoods. And that is one of the first things that I will work toward if I am elected as your new governor. Tighter gun control!"

David Huggins got quiet, looking around the auditorium at the reactions to his words. "But I have a problem. Before I can be elected, before I can begin the healing to our great state, I must win this first battle. I must be appointed as your candidate. The conservatives want to take over our liberal great state. We need to have strong ammunition to fight back. You must remember this." He nodded at the audience and threw up his hands as if in resignation. "The rest is up to you. Thank you."

As he walked off the stage, Huggins looked toward Larry Whitten, his assistant, and smiled. He knew that staying away from political issues and focusing on the domestics would be the key to his victory. Now the results remained to be seen. The problem was he still had some key players who were standing in his way of winning the nomination. They would be taken care of.

"Great job, David," Larry Whitten whispered as David walked by.

"As always," David said with a grin. He shook hands with some of the political associates who vied for his attention.

"Great job, Senator," someone said.

"You're my candidate, Senator Huggins," someone else congratulated.

The accolades went on and on. David Huggins smiled brightly and made his way to the men's bathroom in the back. He took a deep breath and looked in the mirror.

"Governor David Huggins," he said out loud. "Sounds good to me."

"Sounds good to me, too," a voice said from the door.

Michael Riley stood at the door, smiling mischievously. "How's it going, David?"

"What are you doing here?" David huffed. He looked around Michael. "And who let you back here?"

"You know by now that nobody has to let me do anything. It's my world, David. Besides, I've come to take you to lunch. We have things to talk about."

"Sure we do, but now is not the time!" David said vehemently.

"Fine. Meet me at Willy's in an hour for dinner. If you aren't there then I'll come to you."

"Willy's? In Queens? I can't be there in an hour, Riley. Be reasonable now!"

David stopped talking when another man walked into the bathroom. Michael Riley moved quickly into a stall, closing the door behind him. He said out loud, as if to himself, "Nothing like a Willy burger," and started humming.

The Rain Forest restaurant was full of happy, hungry patrons. Most seemed oblivious to their beautiful surroundings. The waters that cascaded down the huge porcelain elephant statues went unnoticed. Unnoticed by all that is, but Kimberla. She sat out in the lobby, looking down at her watch and patting her feet. Delphi was late. She had called and made arrangements for them to have lunch, telling her that she needed a girl pal in New York, and that she was going to adopt her.

"Hmm," she hummed to herself. "Where is that girl?"

She needed Delphi. She hoped that a friendship with her would get her some of the information she needed to help find Margo. There was something about her that told Kimberla that Delphi was a full water bucket waiting to spill.

Looking down at her watch again she was just about ready to give up. She sighed. "Okay, phase two. I guess she changed her mind."

Figuring she would just go in and order some Jungle Ribs to go, Kimberla stood up to go back into the restaurant. She would just have to find another opportunity to talk to Delphi. She had almost made it to the entry door, when she heard wheels squealing to a stop beside her. Delphi jumped out the back of a yellow cab. Her hair was wild and flying in all different directions. As she got closer, Kimberla noticed something else. She had a bruise under her left eye that was carefully concealed with makeup.

"Kimberla, I'm so sorry I'm late!"

"What happened?"

"Well," Delphi said, "I just got caught up at the club and then I needed to go home and get changed, because I didn't bring anything to change in, and it was just all crazy."

"Hmm . . ." Kimberla hummed. She put her hand across Delphi's shoulder. "Well, let's get something to eat. I'm starved."

It didn't take long for them to be seated, which surprised Kimberla since their table had been held so long. She figured it had been given to someone else. She cleared her throat as she looked over the menu. Delphi was very quiet.

"Are you okay, girl?"

Delphi gave her a fake smile. "Sure I am. I just can't decide what I want to eat."

"That's a pretty bruise you have there."

Delphi reached up and touched her eye.

"You mean this little thing? Girl, I hit my eye coming out the kitchen this morning. It's nothing." She laughed weakly.

"It doesn't look like nothing, Delphi." Kimberla leaned closer to her. "Who hit you?" she whispered.

"Nobody hit me. I told you I hit my eye on the door coming out of the kitchen. Damn, what is this?"

She was getting irritated, obviously. That's not what Kimberla wanted. What she needed was for Delphi to trust her.

She thought for a moment before she spoke again, smiling as she asked, "So, what do you have a taste for today? I heard the wings are delicious. Have you ever been here before?"

Delphi didn't answer her, since at that moment their waitress brought their waters over and was ready to take their order. Kimberla opted for the hot wings and tossed salad, and Delphi ordered stuffed mushrooms and salad. They both ordered chocolate liquor with mint. After the waitress left, Kimberla gave Delphi a soft reassuring look.

"I really want us to be friends, Delphi. It's hard living in a new city and not knowing anyone." She reached her hand out. "How about a truce? I wasn't trying to upset you."

Delphi grabbed her hand, took a deep breath, closed her eyes, and then opened them. They were filled with tears.

"You were right. I don't know what to do, Alisha," she said sadly.

"Just tell me what happened."

"It was Michael . . ."

"I figured that." Kimberla nodded. "So, do you want to tell me what happened?"

"Girl, you don't know Michael. I feel bad telling you all this because you're new and I don't want you thinking things, but then again, the other girls at the club are all scared of him or they're blinded by his charm."

"But why did he hit you?" Kimberla asked, leaning forward.

Delphi hesitated. Kimberla knew why. She didn't know her and wasn't sure she could trust her. She just would wait it out and hope that the calm look on her face was convincing enough for her. Suddenly words seemed to pour out of Delphi's mouth. "Michael and I . . . well, we are kind of involved."

"Romantically you mean?"

"Well, I don't know if Michael would describe it as romantic." Delphi laughed. "Maybe sexually; yes, we are sexually involved as far as he is concerned. Me, well I don't know. I don't know why I bother."

"Delphi, I'm not trying to be a fake Ann Landers or be your therapist, but woman-to-woman I have to say this. If you know that it's just sexual, and if, from what you are telling me, you aren't happy with him or with the relationship, why are you in it?"

"Girl, please. Why are any of us always chasing after men who don't want us?" Delphi laughed. "The truth is it didn't start with me wanting Michael. He has a way of convincing others to do as he wants. At first he came after me as if he was interested in me in a romantic way. Eventually I realized he just wanted sex. By that time I had learned other things about him that had me worried, but still, I somehow couldn't pull away. Somehow he had me hooked. Hooked to what I don't know . . ."

A lightbulb went off in Kimberla's head. "What kind of things did you learn about him?"

"For one thing he's into, I mean into . . ." Delphie paused. "I think I'm telling you too much."

Uh-oh, Kimberla thought, *I really don't want to push her away.* She fixed her face with an understanding smile. "Then we can talk about something else. How about you tell me where I can find some tight leather boots for my next set?"

Delphi smiled, seeming relieved at the change of subject. "Okay, I can do that. One thing I do know about is shopping. Now . . . how hot do you want them?"

"Sizzling, girl, sizzling!"

They both laughed, and Kimberla felt relieved that at least for the moment she still had a bit of Delphi's confidence.

But she knew she had a long way to go.

Willie's was New York. Everything about it was New York. The wooden chairs and the umbrellas that stood as heaven over the tiny café tables all testified to its surroundings. The smell of foot-long hot dogs and imported cigars filled the smoggy atmosphere.

The air wasn't the only thing that was smoking. Self-confidence flowed through the pores of Michael Riley. And it was evident to anyone who met him. Senator David Huggins didn't allow that confidence to affect his anger as he sat across from Michael at the small café table.

"What would possess you to pull a trick like that? You could fuck up everything I have going if anyone ever thought I was involved with the likes of you."

Michael laughed. "I was just grabbing an opportunity to hear the great, renowned Senator Huggins's soon-to-be famous speech. I am a taxpaying, voting citizen you know."

"No, what you are is a snake," David Huggins spat angrily. "That wasn't funny, at all. You're screwing up, Riley."

Michael took a puff from his cigar then leaned his elbows on the table. He moved his head to the side and spat out the bits of tobacco that had fallen from his tightly packed cigar. "Enough about all that," he said. "I need to know the shipment dates."

Senator Huggins cleared his throat. "Well, you may as well know we have a slight problem with that."

"What kind of problem?"

"I still have a block in my corner. Ralph Carson is another thorn in my side. He is holding back his bid and he has to be dealt with before I finalize things with you."

"Look, David, if you are having problems with your fellow scumbag politicians, that's your business. I've done everything my side of the bargain here. Now it's time for you to live up to your word."

David Huggins smiled. He took a sip of his ice tea and then motioned to the waitress. She walked over immediately. "I'll have a slice of that Key Lime pie you mentioned." As the waitress nodded then walked away, Huggins turned his attention back toward Michael. "Fact of the matter is, Michael, without me you have no product; without product you have nothing to sell, and without something to sell, you have no business. So it's the simple fact that unless you help me get *all* my stumbling blocks out the way you will always be just another wannabe star with no light. You screwed up before. That was not my fault. We agreed to help each other but I can't continue to help you unless I get into office and you know it."

Michael was silent, but amusement was evident on his face. He shook his head slowly, and then started clapping his hands in applause. "You are good, Senator; props to you. Now explain to me why you feel I would ever let you threaten me? Don't you know me by now?"

"I'm not . . . I'm not threatening you," David Huggins stammered. "But we had an agreement, Michael. Carson has to be dealt with. Surely you can understand that?"

"What you need to understand is that if you need something, you step to me correct, and we can talk. But watch your tone." Michael's eyebrow rose. "You understand?" He sat back comfortably as David Huggins gave him a sheepish nod. "Hmm . . . Okay, tell me about him."

"He is endorsing Kelley Watson. Kelley Watson of all people. Last-minute decision I suppose. She's a semiconservative bitch. I don't know why he would vouch for her, but his mind needs to be changed."

"To be honest, I could care less about that. I don't want to know about Kelley Watson, I want to know about Ralph Carson," Michael said sarcastically. "I want to know about him personally. Frankly, David, I'm getting very bored with these little problems of yours; these little people problems. Let's just get it out of the way and move on."

"Carson likes men," he said abruptly. "I *don't* want him killed. I want him scared into submission. As I told you before, we don't need another Alan Mitchell disaster on our hands."

"That's another story altogether. You, David, are supposed to keep tabs on the FBI. That agent shouldn't have been allowed to bother me. So where is your part of the deal?"

"How can I know everything the Feds are up to?" David Huggins hissed.

"So if you know you can't keep up with everything they are

doing, how do you figure I can?" Michael paused. "Back to this Carson person. You say he likes men?"

"He's a sissy in disguise. So?"

"So, leave it up to me. Like Whitney Houston says, I'll give him all the man he will ever need."

7

New York City

Jacob grabbed Lia's backside, squeezing it as she bounced up and down on top of him. He moaned as she gripped him inside her sugar walls.

"Dayum, baby, shit . . ." he panted.

"Feels good, boo? Feels good, don't it?"

"Hell yeah!"

"Mmm . . ." Lia purred, as she squeezed his manhood again with her walls. She pressed downward, catching her breath as tingles of pleasure surged through her. She leaned forward. "Suck my tits, Jon-Jon, suck 'em, boo!"

He was happy to oblige, sucking her erect nipple in his mouth. The harder he sucked the faster and deeper Lia purged herself up and down his rod. She was a hot number, always had been, and this time was no different. Forget the fact that Lia was everybody's hot number, that didn't concern Jacob much. When old man horny called for a fix, a brotha had to get it any way he could. And the old man was screaming like a mutha when Lia tapped at Jacob's door.

"That's it, Jonathon! Right there. There! Ooh, baby, yes!"

Hearing her grunts and moans, Jacob could tell that Lia was

about to hit that big O. Her high yellow complexion turned a deep hue of red. Chill bumps coated her skin. Her lips quivered as she came in a silent rush. Jacob thrust hard into her one last time before feeling his own orgasm sweep through him.

"Dayum, girl," he coughed out minutes later, fighting to catch his breath.

Lia laughed, then jumped up from his body, her heavy breasts bouncing at attention. "You really know how to please a sistah. Mmm . . ." She reached down, kissing him softly on the lips.

"You're not bad yourself, shawty girl. Now, why don't you jump in the shower real quick and get rolling so I can get some work done."

Lia looked at him in disbelief. "You are so wack. Do you always fuck a lady and then send her on her way? That is so messed up!"

Laughing to himself, Jacob thought how wack she really would think he was if she knew that he didn't consider her to be a lady, at all. He stood up, grabbing his robe, and slipped it on quickly.

"You have to remember something, Lia. Everyone who wears the uniform is not a professional."

"And what does that suppose to mean?" Lia asked, making a face.

"You're a smart girl." Jacob smiled. "Figure it out." He could hear Lia mumbling to herself as she made her way to the bathroom.

Laughing out loud, Jacob started clearing away the evidence of their sex session from the couch, straightening the pillows and gathering the blanket that was scattered there. He was making his way to the bathroom when he heard a soft tap at his door. Looking out the peephole he saw with shock that it was Kimberla Bacon.

"Okay," he whispered. "Now what could she want?" He opened the door slowly.

"Hello, Mr. Simmons." She smirked. "Not!"

"Shh!"

"What?" she queried.

"What do you want?" Jacob whispered.

Kimberla pushed her way through the door. "Since you are so rude and won't invite me in, I'll just invite myself."

Jacob sighed.

"I just need to talk to you, okay?" Kimberla noticed but didn't understand Jacob's antsiness, or why he kept looking around himself. She shrugged her shoulders and continued her thought. "I had lunch with Delphi, she said—"

Grabbing her roughly, Jacob silenced her as he glued his lips to hers. Kimberla fought it for a moment, until his warm, moist lips got the better of her. She melted against him.

The intensity of their kiss took Jacob by surprise, too. This could become habit forming. He felt his heart beating rapidly, and even after just sharing a heated romp with Lia, his body hardened against Kimberla's abdomen. He heard her moan softly as he pulled away from her. His eyes lowered to her mouth, noting the wetness of her tongue as she nervously licked her kiss-bruised lips.

"You know, I'm starting to think we should just fuck and get it over with," he whispered.

That was like a cold glass of water to Kimberla. She gasped angrily and pushed him away from her.

"What the hell is this?"

Both Kimberla and Jacob turned quickly to Lia's demanding voice.

"I said, *what the hell is this!*" she screamed.

Jacob stepped to the plate. "Lia, you don't have a right to question anything I do."

"Bullshit! You just finished doing the do with me and now I come in here and you swapping spit with this skinny hoe?"

Kimberla cleared her throat. Jacob didn't have to look at her to know she was ready to give Lia a royal beat down. One thing he did remember about Kimberla was her quick temper. She could whip ass. Even most men weren't safe if they came at her wrong. He looked toward her and saw that she was about to jump at Lia. Moving quickly, he yanked her back.

"No, don't hold me. I'm gonna show her what this skinny hoe can do!"

"No, Alisha," he said, quickly remembering her alias. "Lia was just leaving. Weren't you, Lia?" Jacob eyed her down. She gave him a stubborn look. *"Weren't you, Lia?"*

"I can't believe this," Lia hissed. "You'll know next time I give you some ass!"

Jacob walked to the door and opened it abruptly. "Bye, Lia."

She rushed to the door, not even noticing Kimberla's foot that had conveniently stuck out, tripping Lia as she passed. Lia fell forward, only missing a fall by Jacob grabbing hold of her. She looked back at Kimberly, accusingly.

"You . . . you—"

Kimberla gave her a wide-eyed, innocent grin.

"Uggg!" Lia spat. "I'll talk to you later, Jonathon," she said, then stormed out of his apartment.

Jacob closed the door quietly behind her, but couldn't close the door to Kimberla's angry eyes.

"Sorry about that."

"Oh, you're sorry? Jacob, why in the world would you have that nasty hoochie mama at your apartment? I hope we aren't gonna have another Hennessy Cooper, T.J. Jackson repeat here."

Jacob laughed and flopped down on the couch. "For one thing, you aren't the chief in charge tonight, Kimberla, okay? And for another, Lia is not a suspect, nor is she under investigation. I don't know of any rule that says an agent can't get busy while on duty."

"Lia Chamberlayne works for Michael Riley, therefore she is part of the coop," Kimberla corrected. Her eyes narrowed as Jacob continued to laugh. "What the hell is so funny?"

"Nothing, it's just . . ." Jacob laid his head back against the sofa, fighting hard to swallow his amusement. "You seem more than just a little jealous, Kimberla . . ."

"Jealous? Jealous of what? You and Lia? Negro, please."

It was hard to know where his bravado was coming from, but for some reason Kimberla's attitude amused Jacob. Even though she was trying to pull rank with her bossiness, he knew that she had none. It felt good to have leverage over her. Or maybe it was the cute pout of her lips when she was upset that turned him on. He paused at the thought. Turned him on? Did Kimberla Bacon, the one and only famed Chameleon, stir his fire? He thought back to their earlier kiss. She definitely roused feelings that even Lia with her rocking hips was not able to light.

"If you come out of the twilight zone I'll tell you why I'm here," Kimberla spat. She still stood looking at him defiantly. Jacob waved his hand for her to continue. He didn't need her to see what he was thinking about, namely, her.

"Okay." Kimberla came and sat down beside him. "As I was starting to say, I talked to Delphi. She had been beat down a little."

That got Jacob's attention. He sat up. "Beat down? What are you talking about?"

"We had lunch earlier. I could tell someone had been slapping her around, although she had attempted to cover it with makeup."

"Mike's handiwork of course . . ."

Kimberla's eyes widened. "You don't sound surprised."

Anyone who knew him knew Mike ran his women with the same iron hand he used to handle his establishments and street vendors. Kimberla was right. Jacob was far from surprised by her revelations. Even though he wasn't and had never been very close to Delphi, it bothered him to know that Mike had been using her for a punching bag. She seemed to be a sweet enough girl. The problem was it was all part of the business. Few women got involved with Michael Riley and were not aware of the cost.

"So, what else did she tell you?" he asked.

"Not much. But the point is I got her to open up. She started getting uncomfortable, but I can tell it will only be a matter of time before I crack her shell. All I have to do is make her feel she can trust me."

"Hmm . . ."

"Jacob! Do you get what I'm saying? Delphi knows every-thing about Michael's business practices. That means she knows about Margo and could perhaps give us something we can pin on this asshole!"

Jacob rubbed his hands over his face, sighing slightly. Kimberla was so determined to get her hands into things.

"Kimberla, Michael Riley is not the one I'm trying to pin."

"What do you mean he's not the one? Don't you think he had something, everything to do with Margo's disappearance?"

"Probably, definitely so," Jacob admitted.

"Well?"

"I'm just saying that pinning him for murder is not the focus of my assignment. Your snooping around is one thing. But once you find the information you're looking for, it won't stop there."

"Oh, it will for me," Kimberla exclaimed. "A federal agent is missing; one who was investigating Mackings. I will get his ass."

Jacob pulled back in surprise. "You will get his ass? Whatever happened to you will find out what happened to Margo, then get your ass back to D.C.?"

"Oh, you know what I meant, Jacob!"

"Don't you think I am just as concerned about Margo Hunter as you are?" Jacob asked, grabbing Kimberla by the shoulders. They both paused, looking into each other's eyes. Jacob could tell that her mind was backtracking to the exact place his was. The kiss. He watched as she licked her lips tentatively.

"I-I don't understand your protest about what I'm saying."

"That's because you don't know what my assignment is. Yes I'm concerned about what happened to Margo, but this is so much bigger than that."

"Then tell me. Tell me so I can understand," she insisted.

Jacob opened his mouth, about to speak when the phone rang. "Hold up."

He walked to the kitchenette and picked it up. "Hello?"

"Jonathon." It was Mario Lincoln.

"Hold up, man."

Jacob looked over at Kimberla. "I'll talk to you later," he whispered.

"But—"

"Later," he insisted.

She sighed, grabbed her purse, and made way for the door.

Ronnie Jones wasn't your average boy next door, although his blond/blue-eyed good looks belied that fact. He was what most would call *pretty*.

As he sat on the black leather couch, he felt irritation taking over him. Time was money, and money was what his time was worth, he thought. He reached in his back pocket and pulled out a pack of Marlboro Reds. His life as a highly paid male prostitute was a lucrative one. It was gigs like this one that paid off the most. He got a call the night before. One-night gig. A quick job. He was to get the senator addicted to the ass, reel him in with the cock, take a few pictures, and be on his way. Sounded easy enough.

Ralph Carson walked in from the bedroom, disrupting Ronnie's thoughts. His dark brown eyes held the same lust that had shone when he first opened the door moments before. He was a short, slightly balding husk of a man.

"So, where were we?" he said, as he sat down beside Ronnie. He reached over, caressing his thigh with his stubby-fingered hand. "You are a top, aren't you?"

"I'm whatever you want me to be," Ronnie responded, slightly bored. This was gonna be a trying trick, he thought. But it's what he got paid for.

Senator Carson licked his lips. "Follow me," he said. He got up and walked back toward the bedroom with Ronnie following close behind.

Once they were there he closed the window blinds and cut on the lamp that sat upon the round bed table.

"Take off your clothes," he demanded. "I want to see all of you."

Ronnie obliged, slowly removing his calico pants and white shirt. He willed himself to think of something that turned him on, like sexy black men. White men did nothing for him, but they were where the money was at and he loved money even more than he craved dark meat.

"Oh my! You look like a Greek god!" Senator Carson exclaimed. He had removed his own clothing. The same could not be said for him, Ronnie lamented to himself. Unclothed, Carson was even more repulsive. He walked to the bed, stretched out over it assed up, and wiggled.

"I want you . . . I need you to fuck me, now!"

8

New York City

Time seemed to be come to a standstill for Kimberla. It had been over a week since she had come to New York, and she knew it wouldn't be long before the Bureau sent someone to infiltrate Mackings. So much was at risk, like her job and her reputation. She needed to work fast. She knew in a way, though, she had to be patient. It was still a fact that with this case she couldn't get juice from a lemon if she squeezed it while it was still cold. She'd have to work it a little; soften it up. And that's what she was trying to do with Delphi and Mackings.

Having a bit of luck, she was able to find a studio apartment in east Manhattan. Jacob said it looked too odd for her to be staying at a fancy hotel in Manhattan yet dancing at Mackings. As she changed in the Mackings dressing room, all she could think was that she wanted to get back to that little hole of an apartment and relax. Maybe then she could think up some way to make her endeavors more successful.

"You did a great job tonight, Alisha," Heaven, one of the dancers, said to her as she passed.

"Thanks!" Kimberla smiled. Heaven was one of the nicer girls of the bunch of cat-howling, bootie-shaking strippers.

After bidding Heaven good night, she grabbed her small changing case and headed out of the dressing room. It was later in the night, and the hallway was vacant and quiet. *The things that go on here must be the best-kept secret in town,* she thought. Just as that thought fled her mind she heard voices coming from Michael Riley's office as she passed. She stopped and listened in.

"He had the audacity to bring it up," Michael said.

"How much does David really know though?" an unfamiliar voice asked.

Who was David? Kimberla thought.

"He knows we had to get rid of her. He knows she was FBI. Other than that he told me on many occasions that he didn't want to know how we did our dirty business," Michael said. "Just like a politician. They want to kick out orders and take the glory for good things, but anything else is just too messy for them. Whether they are the one ordering the hit or not," Michael Riley said, laughing.

"That's true . . . So, what did you do with the body?"

Body? Oh my God, Margo! Kimberla felt her heart beat at a rapid pitch. She had always worried and been concerned; she had known deep in her heart that Margo had to be dead, but to hear the words brought hot tears to her eyes. She swallowed deeply and was about to listen for more information when she heard footsteps coming up the hallway behind her.

Clutching her bag close to her, she hurried away from Michael's door and took the double-doored exit from the club. The doors were locked. Jones appeared suddenly, smiling his ever-ready cocky grin.

"You sure got my attention tonight, Chameleon," he said, winking. Kimberla felt disconcerted, something that was new for her. She always had her head clear and straight, regardless of the situation put before her. But the revelation about Margo had her spinning in a mind-dazing circle.

"What do you mean?" she stammered.

"I *liked* your striptease. Don't you understand what I mean now?" Jones laughed salaciously.

Ugh, Kimberla thought. Jones was one of the many things

she didn't like about her stripper/dancer alias. In fact, the dancing, which had seemed kind of daring and fun a week ago, was now irritating the hell out of her. She figured it was because of the *not getting anywhere* feeling she had been having.

"Good night, Jones," Kimberla said with emphasis, rolling her eyes.

He laughed at her back as she walked out the building and hailed a cab.

As the cab made its way down the busy streets of Queens, Kimberla closed her eyes and thought about Margo. She hadn't seen her in two months, but she could still remember their last conversation; she could still hear her voice . . .

"I thought you weren't going to take another assignment until after your wedding?" Kimberla reminded her, as they lounged by the fireplace, sipping rum-laced coffees.

"Well, I wasn't at first," Margo said, *"but you know I'm always down for a challenge."* She winked.

"A challenge is one thing, suicide is another. You're gonna kill yourself, Margo."

"With work?" Margo laughed.

Kimberla groaned as the hot liquor flowed through her. She was feeling a little tipsy.

"Well, maybe. But you know I feel a dang-on man will kill you first. Them childish, needy, pain in da ass mens!"

Margo fell out laughing. *"You're right about that!"* She brought her coffee cup up to Kimberla's for a toast. *"And if anyone can drive me to the grave, it would be a man. But I know that would never happen to you."*

"It sure wouldn't. You know all a man can do for me is scratch my back, suck my toes, give me the big O, and get the hell on," Kimberla joked as she bumped cups with her girlfriend. *"If any ever tried to tie me down like Frem is doing you, I'd karate-five-O their butt."*

"Okay, so let's make a deal, since you are my one and only bestest friend in the world—"

"There is no such word as bestest, Margo." Kimberla chuckled.

"I have my own dialect, now hush up and listen. As I was saying, since you are my bestest friend in the world, if Frem or any man ever tried to hurt me, I expect you to turn into a female Jackie Chan and karate-five-O their masculine behinds. So don't forget, or I'll come back from the grave and haunt you!"

They had both laughed. She could still hear the laughter. But she would never forget the promise made in jest. She couldn't and she wouldn't. She would find out who had hurt Margo. She would find out what had happened to her, even if it took all eternity.

"Unbelievable."

"What's unbelievable?"

Jacob smiled as he looked around Kimberla's small but cozy apartment. "For the first time since you've been to New York, you've actually listened to something I had to say."

Kimberla seemed to be ignoring his sarcasm. She walked to her kitchenette, opened the fridge, and pulled out two Heineken beers.

"I heard something today," she said, as she sat Indian style on the floor.

"You danced tonight, right?"

"Yes."

"So, what did you hear?"

Taking a gulp of her beer, her face took on a serious, sad expression. "I heard Michael talking in his office to someone. I know they were talking about Margo. He said something about having killed the FBI agent . . ."

"Margo . . ." Jacob said slowly.

"Yes," Kimberla croaked. She closed her eyes. "Are you gonna help me?"

He wasn't surprised. Unbeknownst to Kimberla, Jacob had heard rumors the day before, from Mario Lincoln of course, about an agent they had to take care of. There was question in his mind about how Michael had found out about Margo's status. A leak perhaps? That wouldn't be anything new. There were always crooked agents who would sell their own souls to the devil for a few extra dollars in their pockets. That's something he would have to figure out in the future. Right now his biggest problem was getting rid of Kimberla. Her jeopardizing his cover could not be tolerated. She was too emotionally involved.

"Come here." Jacob nodded to her.

"What?"

He nodded a gesture again. Until, finally, Kimberla knee-walked up to the sofa. Putting both hands on her shoulders he said, "You need to go back to D.C., or else Maryland to see your father like you planned. Now that you know what's happened to Margo there is no reason for you stay any longer." Kimberla started shaking her head even before Jacob had finished talking. "Listen to me, Kimberla. You are jeopardizing your job. You realize that don't you? And mine, too, for not spilling the beans on you."

"Don't you think I know that? I . . . I'll leave as soon as . . ."

"As soon as what?" he demanded.

"As soon as I find out what happened to her."

"Ugh, woman. You never change, do you? You're still the same stubborn-ass female you were in college!"

"Hmph!" Kimberla exclaimed. She looked down at her hands for a moment. "I'm not going to do anything to hurt you, Jacob. I hope you know that. If you want to disassociate yourself from me while I'm here, I understand."

Jacob looked at her solemnly for a moment. "Damn. You know I can't do that. I can't just leave you to your own devices. Lord knows what trouble you'll get yourself into."

"I can take care of myself, Agent White." She laughed at his audacity.

"I don't care how tough you are, or how tough you think you are. You know that Margo Hunter is probably dead. The same thing can happen to you. I won't have you on my conscience."

"One more week," Kimberla said, choking a bit on her words. "Let me check things out for one more week. I swear if I don't at least find out what they did to her by then, I'll leave and let Washington handle it. I do love my job, contrary to what you are thinking. I don't plan on being fired over this. I don't want to jeopardize your cover either. I'll talk to Kyte Williams when I get to Maryland. I don't necessarily need to tell him I was here, but he knows me, so any information I get my hands on I will forward to him and just tell him I had my own people checking into things, okay?"

"You promise?" Jacob didn't trust that glint in her eyes. Does a zebra ever shed his stripes?

"Scout's honor," Kimberla said, making a cross-your-heart sign on her chest. Jacob wondered if her toes were crossed, too.

"Okay," he finally said. "In the meanwhile, I think we should start acting a bit more convincingly that we have a love jones going on."

"Why?" she almost shouted. Jacob laughed.

"Damn, is it that horrible?"

"Is what?" she coughed out.

"Pretending to be my . . . boo."

Kimberla thought for a moment. "I think you just want to get into my panties." She smiled.

He wasn't denying it. The Kimberla Bacon he knew in college had evolved into a sexy somebody. But still . . .

"There has to be some reason for you and me to be spending so much time together. We have to be smart with this you know. Besides, Mike already believes I have my eye on you."

"Will you tell me what your assignment is? You keep saying that Michael is not the gist of it."

"He's not."

Jacob sighed. "I just don't want you trying to hang around too long and I know that's what you'll try to do, woman."

"Just tell me how much it has to do with Margo."

"It has nothing to do with her. That's just it. If it did then she and I would have been working together and we weren't."

"So why was she here?"

"I don't know, Kimberla. That's just it."

Kimberla was quiet. Damn her curiosity, Jacob thought. He knew what her next question would be.

"Okay, so will you help me find that out?"

"Will you keep your word and leave if I do?" His heart was racing, waiting for her answer. "Well?

Kimberla smiled again. "Okay, *boo*."

He didn't believe her, not for a moment. He looked at her and frowned. She was going to be a problem.

9

The club was full for a Thursday night, almost as if it were the weekend. The dressing room was even fuller. Kimberla was talking with Delphi about her last set. She had noticed how slow Delphi was moving, and was a bit concerned that Michael had been using her as a punching bag again. Suddenly the door flew open. Speak of the devil, Kimberla thought. He walked in smiling.

"Ladies, ladies; you all are hot tonight!" he sung.

The dancers giggled, all but for Kimberla who smiled at him sweetly, and Delphi, whose face had gone bland the moment Michael walked into the room. Kimberla understood her reaction. Ever since she heard Michael discussing how he had to get rid of the *agent,* she had to fight tooth and nail with her alter ego that wanted to skin his ass alive, literally. She fought hard to keep the smile believable on her face.

"How are you, Alisha?" he asked.

"I'm fine, thanks."

Michael nodded, looking at her oddly. "I want to talk to you for a moment." He gestured toward the door. "The rest of you, leave."

The other ladies murmured nosily around the room. None of them could be even half as curious as Kimberla was, though. Wondering what Michael could want. She half worried that he may have found out she was listening outside his door the night before. She muddled inside her head while the other ladies left, trying to think of a good excuse she could give.

Instead of leaving, Lia, who had just come out of the bathroom, walked up to Michael, caressing his cheek with her long nailed fingers. He grabbed her hand.

"You, too, Lia."

"But, Michael—"

"Leave," he demanded, stopping her in her tracks before she started her begging campaign.

Kimberla coughed back a chuckle. She couldn't help it. Lia was so pitiful. She turned around and looked at Kimberla, her eyes shooting sparks, and stormed out the door behind the other girls.

"Somebody is not too happy with you, it seems," Michael noted with amusement.

"I guess not. But then again, jealousy is a mutha." She smirked.

"So says the queen! So, how do you like it here so far?"

"Well it's been great," she responded, still feeling on edge.

"The money isn't bad either, is it?"

"No." Kimberla laughed. "The gentlemen at Mackings are very generous, and so are you."

Michael looked at her oddly and leaned against one of the dressing tables. Kimberla felt suddenly as if the room were closing in on her. What did he do to Margo? What kind of man was he really? Behind the classy manners and fancy suits, she feared she was dallying with Satan himself.

"How would you like to make a few more dollars, on the side?" he finally asked her.

He really caught her attention with that. Was he letting her in on something deeper within his organization?

"How can I do that?" Kimberla asked.

Easing into one of the swinging chairs by the two-way mirrors, Michael sat down and pulled a cigarette out of the gold case he kept in his shirt pocket. Kimberla gagged inwardly. *Why did people always have to push their nicotine death wish upon helpless people who loved to breathe fresh air?*

"I have a spot that not too many people know about. It's called The Dorm. It's a party palace. A few of the girls stay there. It also would save you because you could actually live there, rent free. So what do you say?"

The pieces were coming together for Kimberla. He was talking about a damn whorehouse. Nah uh, no way. Change her skins again? Not that much. How could she ever pretend to be a hoe without giving up the goods for real?

"I don't think so, Michael. I'm pretty content where I am now. I just got a new place and it's affordable. But thanks for thinking about me though."

"Whoa!" He laughed. "You turned that down fast."

"Only because I kind of know what you're asking. I'm only doing this temporarily to earn money for dance school. I'm not trying to make a career out of taking off my clothes. And I sure as hell won't be fucking for money."

Michael blew smoke out his nostrils, and smiled seductively. "Who said anything about fucking?"

"Isn't that what we're talking about? A whorehouse?"

"Ouch! Such a nasty word. Do I look like a pimp to you? I've far too much class for that. I'm talking escorts here. Very clean, classy, sexy. And no, you don't have to fuck anybody that you don't want to. It would be completely up to you. You would just be spending time and working as an escort to rich, distinguished gentlemen who love the company of beautiful women. That's all."

Hell no! Kimberla thought. "I don't know," she said out loud. "I don't think so."

"Well, just think about it, okay?"

Kimberla was quiet as Michael walked to the door. He turned and smiled at her again. "Think about it," he said again, rubbing his point finger and thumb together as if to signify money. As he turned to open the door, there was a knock. He opened it quickly and there stood Jacob.

"Jonathon!" Michael exclaimed. "To what do I owe this visit?"

"Oh," Jacob stammered. "I was looking for Alisha. One of the girls said she was still in here changing."

"You were looking for her? For what, if I may ask?"

Kimberla gave Jacob a worried look, and swallowed hard. He threw a kiss at her.

Michael looked from Jacob to Kimberla, and raised his eyebrows. "So, that's what's up. Are you two kickin' it now? Alisha, I hope you aren't fucking just to be fucking. I know how you said you felt about that," he joked.

He walked past Jacob. "Don't let her break ya heart, brother. She's dangerous," he said with a wink. Then patted him on the back and made his way down the hall.

Ralph Carson fell back against the plush pillows, breathless. His stout body felt sated. He could still feel the pleasurable tingles coursing through him that had his soul kissing the heavens moments before.

He watched as Ronnie Jones, his sexual savior, dressed languidly after having just showered. Ralph didn't have the energy to shower. He didn't want to wash Ronnie's scent off any sooner than was necessary. Hooked was the only word to describe how he felt about the young prostitute. He didn't have any illusions of love. Ronnie held one purpose and one purpose only. But he was starting to feel this unexplainable craving for the young man.

"You're incredible," he whispered sensuously.

"Oh yeah? Glad you approve," Ronnie said back. He yawned and slipped his shirt over his head. His blond hair was still moist from his shower.

"Oh, I definitely approve. You really know how to work your sexy body."

His back turned to the senator, Ronnie frowned in distaste, then finally turned around and fixed a smile on his face. "Well like I said, I aim to please. I really hate to stick and run, but I have another client."

"You do?" Ralph Carson asked.

"Yup."

Ralph cleared his throat. He felt uneasiness come over him. This handsome, evasive young man was getting to him. He didn't like the idea of sharing him with other men. He knew he couldn't afford for it to ever be found out that he was gay, but Ronnie seemed to be just what he was looking for. He was discreet, sexy, urban yet not too street. The perfect boy toy.

"So, I'll talk to you later," Ronnie said as he hooked his cell phone to his hip.

"Wait! I need . . . I need to know something . . ."

Ronnie looked at him curiously.

The senator took a deep breath, swallowing convulsively. "What would it cost me to keep you?"

Ronnie paused for a moment before speaking. "Keep me? Look, man, Ronnie doesn't get kept by anyone. I'm my own man. I do my thing." He got up to leave.

"Wait," Senator Carson exclaimed. He got up quickly. His stomach jiggled as he pranced over to Ronnie. "You have to understand a man in my position. I have needs, but I can't take chances with my political career. Someone like you could do well, having a friend like me."

"I have plenty of friends."

"And I have plenty of connections." Ralph looked at him with a quiet intensity. "I know you don't want to be turning tricks the rest of your life, Ronnie. Let me do things for you. Good things."

"And what do I have to do for you?" Ronnie asked sarcastically.

Ralph reached out, touching Ronnie's cheek tenderly. "See no one but me; let me take care of you." He squeezed Ronnie's shoulder. "You . . . would belong to me. And you will never want for anything."

Ronnie eyed him warily. "You hold that thought. I'll let you know." He reached over to the dresser, grabbed his keys, and walked out of the room.

*   *   *

An hour later Ralph Carson sat at his desk with his navy blue satin robe on, clicking away at his computer. The relaxed, sexually charged feeling he had earlier was gone. He was the type of man who usually got what he wanted. Even though Ronnie appealed to him with his rough, conceited, yet tender personality, Ralph was vexed by the boy holding back on his offer. He figured only a fool would turn down anything that was financially rewarding. There was always a fool's paradise though, Ralph just had to show Ronnie the way to it.

At this thought his phone rang. He looked at the clock and noticed it was after midnight. "Hello?" he said quickly.

"Hello, Senator Carson."

"Who is this?" Ralph asked.

There was a laugh. "I'm disappointed, my friend."

"David?"

"Bingo. How's it going?" David Huggins asked.

"How is what going, David?"

"Life." David laughed. "You know why I'm calling you. It's getting close to the deadline for bids. I thought with our being old friends you would let me in on what yours will be."

"You know damn well what my bid is. I will not be a part of helping a man like you get in office. You're not fit to be governor, David. You know it and I know it." Ralph could barely conceal the irritation in his voice.

"That's a pity. I had hoped you'd reconsider," he said lazily.

"No, I will *not* reconsider," Ralph said with finality.

"Again, that's a pity. I'll talk to you later." Ralph was about to hang up, before David grabbed his attention again. "Oh, by the way, how's your sex life?"

"My . . . my what?" Ralph whispered.

David laughed again. "Your sex life, my friend."

David Huggins laughed at Ralph's shocked gasp, and hung up the phone.

Traffic was heavy. Jacob could tell that Kimberla was tired. With all the prancing she had been doing lately on stage it wasn't surprising. He laughed to himself. She seemed to be enjoying her little stripper masquerade a bit too much. He watched from the corner of his eye as she feigned sleep.

"Wake up, sleeping beauty," he crooned out.

"I'm not asleep." She laughed. She stretched and yawned. "Thanks for picking me up tonight. I'm getting so tired of cabs."

"I thought you would appreciate it," Jacob said softly. "So, what was going on with you and Michael? He seemed to be in a jovial mood."

"Oh, I had just finished making love to him."

Mouth flying open, Jacob's eyes widened in shock. Kimberla burst out laughing.

"I'm kidding, idiot!"

"You'd best be. Remember you're supposed to be *my* lady."

Kimberla seemed to ignore his comment.

"Tell me something," she finally said, "have you ever heard of a place called The Dorm?"

"Michael asked you to escort at The Dorm," Jacob stated knowingly. "Damn, girl, he must really be impressed with you!"

"Get off of that and just tell me about the place, okay?"

"The Dorm is Michael's pride and joy. He has only the best ladies work there—the most beautiful. It's an escort house where rich men are catered to."

"And sex?"

Jacob smirked. "That's never discussed. Come on, Kimberla, do you think Michael Riley is stupid? I've dealt with him for a year. If there is one thing I've learned about him it's that he is intelligent."

"You sound almost like a fan," Kimberla stated, looking at Jacob oddly.

"Well, I'm always a fan to intelligence. But there is one thing I know about people like that: sometimes you can outsmart yourself. I'm betting on him doing that. He feels he can trust me now. He's letting me in on things that he's always kept under wraps."

"Like what type of things?"

She thought she was slick. Jacob laughed. "None of your business."

"Hmph."

They drove in silence for a while. Jacob's eyes kept drawing to Kimberla. Her skin seemed to sparkle, and the contacts she wore were flattering to her. He found himself thinking about her more and more, even when she was not around. He wasn't sure what that could mean, but his mind hadn't been so preoccupied with a woman since his wife.

"You're looking extra lovely tonight . . ."

Kimberla blushed. "That's a nice compliment coming from you."

"As if you don't get compliments."

"Well you know at Georgetown I wasn't exactly the queen of hearts. I got no play from guys like you."

"And what kind of guy was I?"

"Negro, please. Let's just say you were the kind that didn't notice me."

Times really do change. Jacob thought back to their GTU days. He was a football player; popular; in love with one of the most beautiful girls on campus; and he had his career goals clear in front of him. Kimberla was more of the athletic type of girls. And even after they finished college and later join the Bureau, she still held that manly aura about herself. Maybe it was the fact that by the time Jacob connected with her again she was already climbing her way to the top. She demanded respect and usually got it. Seeing her now in her new feminine role was catching him off guard. He had to believe that was the reason for his mental preoccupation with her.

"You're mighty quiet over there," Kimberla said, breaking into his thoughts.

Jacob swallowed hard, parked his vehicle in front of Kimberla's apartment building, and turned to her. Their eyes held for the briefest of moments before he reached out to trace her lips with his fingers. He felt a tender electricity surge through them, and pulled back as Kimberla caught her breath. He decided to change the subject.

"I was just thinking about how I got here. FBI work was not my initial career dream as you know."

"I kind of knew that. You know, Jacob, I always wondered what made you join the Bureau."

Jacob was quiet for a moment, wondering how much of himself and his inner feelings he should reveal to her. He opened and closed his mouth a few times before, for some reason, he felt himself opening up. He laid his head back against the bucket seats and began to speak.

"After Regina and Bali were killed, I felt lost for a while. I didn't know what I wanted to do with my life but I did know private investigation was no longer going to be a part of it." He took a deep breath and continued, not even aware if Kimberla was listening or not. He was lost in his own painful world of memories.

"Tell me what happened, Jacob," Kimberla said softly. She laid her hand on his arm, squeezing slightly.

"Bali had a fever when I left that morning. She had been battling a cold that whole week. Regina said she would be okay so I went on to work." He paused. "Regina took her to the doctor's alone. And on the way back they stopped at Krispy Kreme's for donuts." He laughed sadly. "Bali loved donies. That's what she called them, you know. They went through the drive-through, and when they pulled off a man stopped in front of the car, put a gun to Regina's head, and forced them both out of the car. Everyone who saw said she didn't put up a fight, but still he shot her. He shot her right in front of witnesses. In broad daylight. I mean, he wasn't even trying to hide it. And then the worst of all, he shot my baby girl, in the street like a dog. For no reason at all." Jacob looked at Kimberla, misty eyed and choking on every word. "She was just three years old, Kimberla. He had no reason to kill her. He had no reason . . ."

Kimberla covered her mouth with her hands. "I'm so sorry, Jacob," she cried. "I'm so sorry."

"After the trial I just needed a new life. But I also needed to be in a position to do something that would help stop this type of thing from happening to anyone else. The boy who killed Regina and Bali was just a go-boy. During the trial I looked into the eyes of that punk nigga who killed my world. But it wasn't him I wanted. It was the people who sent him. He worked for a group of carjackers. There is always someone who is the root culprit. FBI work was the only way to get to the source. It's what I want; what I need . . ." His voice trailed off. He didn't even realize that his hands were holding the steering wheel so tight till he felt Kimberla loosening them.

As her hands held his he somehow knew she understood. He buried his face in her neck and exhaled.

10

Brooklyn, New York

The hummingbird usually tells you what time of day it is. With its musical lyrics and magical hymns, the sleep mask of the night is woken. In the dawn of day all that seemed so terrible the night before has another chance. At least that's what we like to believe. Every day is a new beginning, a fresh start.

Kimberla's fresh start hadn't yet begun. She was in a death-like slumber. The phone rang beside her, once, twice, three times, yet still she slept. On the fourth ring she opened one eye. The sound of the phone was almost angry. She suddenly grabbed the receiver in a rush.

"Hello?"

"What the hell are you doing in New York?"

Kimberla's heart skipped a beat. "Kyte? How did you get this number?"

"Don't worry about how I got the number. What are you doing in New York? What have you been up to, Kim?"

There wasn't enough speed in the span of time for Kimberla to come up with a good enough reason for her actions. Her mind was racing, but she decided she would just tell the truth.

"Kyte, you know I wanted to talk to you about this. I have

some leads about Margo. I wanted to make sure I had enough to help you guys on the case before I called you, though." Kyte's silence worried Kimberla. "Are you there?"

She could sense his anger. She wasn't sure how on the line her job was at the moment, but even with that at stake, Kimberla couldn't see herself leaving before she got the answers she sought.

"Yes, I'm here. So why did you feel you had to interlope into things like this? Do you feel I couldn't handle it?" Kyte asked.

"No, not you, Kyte. But I do know that with Malcolm Johnson being on the case . . . Well, I just don't trust him."

"You mean to tell me you're willing to risk the career you've spent years building to satisfy some silly vendetta with Malcolm Johnson? Kimberla, come on, this doesn't seem like you!" Kyte Williams huffed.

"Kyte . . ." Kimberla whispered, "Margo is dead." There was silence on the other end. "Did you hear me?"

"How did you find that out?"

He didn't seem surprised.

"I heard Michael Riley talking about her. He owns the club she was working at."

"Mackings?"

"Yes."

Kyte sighed. "What else have you found out?"

She sat up in the bed. Stretching slightly, she looked around for her robe. She grabbed it and slipped it over her shoulders, then slipped her feet into her satin bedroom slippers. "That's just the point. I feel there is something more going on here. For one, I haven't exactly heard her name. But I have made a connection with one of the dancers and if I can give it a few days, I'm sure eventually she will tell me what she knows. She's already told me that Michael Riley is into some things that are not quite legal. Kyte . . ." Kimberla closed her eyes before continuing.

"Are you there?" he called.

"Yes. I know I overstepped my bounds coming here. I can understand you being upset with me."

"My being upset with you isn't the problem. Your being in

danger is. There's a lot about this case you don't know. Malcolm is sending Agent Micah Latimer to New York. Having too many agents on this case can cause a problem and jeopardize the investigation."

"Why is Latimer coming here?" she stormed.

"Kim." Kyte laughed. "Once again, you seem to forget this is not your case. It's Malcolm Johnson's. And whether you like him or not isn't the issue here. He's assigned Micah Latimer."

"So, you want me to come back to D.C.?" Kimberla asked flatly. "Just leave everything and all the doors I've opened?"

"Actually, no. That would be detrimental at this point. You are already visible. To take you off the case now would risk everything. But Latimer will be in on this case and you will work with him, and that's final."

Micah Latimer. Kimberla had worked with him before, but never in a close nature. He was a pretty-boy brother, on the quiet side, but from what she could remember, very dedicated and serious about his job. Now her mind was working overtime wondering how he would affect her investigation. It's funny that she called it her investigation, the fact being again, as Kyte just said, it was not her assignment, but just one she had jumped into on her own. But the hell with that, Kimberla thought. She wasn't some wimpy-ass chick who waited for green lights. She had made it her own.

"Because I love and respect you, Kim, I'm going to forget this serious mishap of yours. But don't you ever let it happen again," Kyte said quietly.

Kimberla swallowed a lump. She knew she was getting off easy.

"I know, Kyte. It's just with this . . . with this I just—"

"I know," he cut in. "Because it's Margo, you couldn't help yourself. I'll make sure you are officially assigned, and I'll be in contact with you when Latimer gets there. You and he need to meet up and go over things. He'll be there by noon tomorrow."

"Thank you so much, Kyte," Kimberla said, feeling much relief.

"Kim, if this operation gets screwed up in any way because

of what you've pulled, it won't be pretty. You're gonna have a lot to answer for."

"Yes," she whispered, "I do know."

Later in the afternoon Kimberla was having one of her favorite quiche dishes at Bistro du Nord. She ate slowly, watching the hordes of patrons indulging in their tasty meals and outward conversations. Suddenly she heard a deafeningly loud cry. She turned around to see a young Asian couple. The man was holding a baby seat carrier, and a loud obvious odor whiffed toward her. Kimberla frowned in distaste. It wasn't that she hated children. They were okay, *in their place,* but Bistro du Nord was not the place for a baby. She decided that as good as her quiche was, she had enough and stood to leave. Her mind was busy thinking about how she would keep Micah Latimer at bay. It's funny that she was worried about him interrupting her investigation. Jacob felt the same way about her interrupting his.

Jacob. After she paid her bill and made her way out of Bistro's, her mind backtracked to the evening before when he had basically poured his heart out to her. Although she always felt Jacob was handsome and extremely sexy, she never knew he was such an amazing man, such a sensitive soul. Her heart bled for the pain she knew he'd gone through in losing his family. That pain was still very much alive in him. Somehow it touched a cord in her that was magnetic.

Kimberla shook herself mentally and continued her cab-grabbing campaign. One thing she wouldn't miss when she finally left New York was hailing cabs. Just as one pulled up, her cell phone did a serenade. She grabbed it from its clip and jumped in the cab.

"Hello," she said, out of breath.

"Alisha! He let me go. Michael let me go!"

Kimberla sat forward in alarm. "Delphi? What do you mean he let you go?"

"Girl, he fired me!" she cried.

"Oh, Delphi. I'm so sorry. Did he say why?"

"Oh, basically because I didn't wanna fuck one of his uppity friends. He's a monster. You hear me? The man is a monster!" Delphi's sniffles became more intense. "You watch yourself with him, Alisha. He's a very bad man. He kills people, sells drugs. Shit, I should go to the police myself. He can't do this to me!"

"How do you know that?" Kimberla whispered. She had her fingers crossed that she may finally be getting Delphi where she wanted her.

"I need my job. I have bills, damn it!" Delphi was on a rambling rampage, then suddenly seemed to realize that Kimberla had asked her a question. "How do I know what?"

"What you just told me."

"You mean that he kills people and is a drug dealer? Girl, I could tell you some shit about Michael that would make your skin crawl. Half the murders and disappearances in New York would point back to him if he didn't have people in high places covering his ass. And I know you are into Jonathon Simmons, but do you ever wonder just what he does for Michael? He sure as hell ain't no stripper. You just be careful with him. You be careful with him and you be careful with Michael. I don't want to see anything happen to you. I really don't."

Kimberla quietly digested all that Delphi was saying. Time was running out. She had to get all she could on Michael Riley while she had a chance. It was time for her to *take* a chance.

"Delphi, where are you right now?" she asked her.

"Now? I'm at my sister's apartment in Crown Heights, why?"

"Get a cab, and meet me at Central Park. We really need to talk . . ."

The life of a politician is one of chance. You win some, you lose some, yet a true winner always comes out on top. For the past two years since he had been in the New York Senate, Ralph Carson had been a winner.

He dallied around his desk at the east Manhattan home he shared with his wife of twenty years. His marriage was a necessity. It wasn't that he didn't love his wife, but his carnal desires were elsewhere. Just the thoughts of the delectable young men he had toyed with over the years hardened his body in sensitive places. One in particular came to mind. That sexy one, Ronnie Jones. Ralph was disappointed that he'd never heard back from him regarding his proposition. He wasn't too worried though. Ronnie was a smart enough kid to know a good thing when he saw it.

"Ralph."

He turned to the sound of his wife's voice.

"I'm trying to work, Laura."

"I just wanted to tell you that UPS is at the door. There's a delivery for you and they won't let me sign for it."

"Oh okay," he said, frowning. He hated being disturbed. Marriage may be a necessity, but it was also a pain in the ass, and so was Laura.

She followed him as he walked to the front door. He turned around, giving her a hostile stare. "Can I walk by myself, please?" he spat.

Laura Carson sighed and then disappeared into the kitchen.

"Sign here," the UPS man said as Ralph opened the screen door.

It was a small package wrapped in brown paper. His curiosity was deeply aroused. Rarely did he get packages delivered at his home. Usually it was at his office or the small apartment he used for his sexual adventures with other men.

Ralph signed the ledger, grabbed the package, and closed the door. He could feel Laura's eyes beaming at his back as he walked back into his office. He turned around, looked at her, and closed the door.

It was a videotape.

"Hmm . . ." he mumbled, slipping it into his VHS player. He locked the door to his office before pushing the ON button.

As the video started, his alarm was instant. The images before him seemed to be in slow motion. His naked body shivering in ecstasy as it was being plundered again and again by Ronnie Jones. Vomit congealed in his throat as he watched himself. The cheap hoe had taped him. He was obviously planning blackmail. Ralph saw all his work, all the years he had spent building his reputation disappearing like smoke. He swallowed deeply as he saw himself ejaculating on his chest and wailing like a woman. He fell back in his leather chair in mental exhaustion, wrapping his arms around himself as chills coursed through him.

The phone rang. He jumped at the blaring sound of it, pausing before answering. Somehow he felt without answering that it would be someone connected to the tape. He took a deep breath and slowly picked up the receiver.

Clearing his throat, he whispered, "Hello . . ."

"Senator Carson, how are you this evening?" an unrecognizable voice asked.

"I'm fine," he croaked.

"Good, good. So, did you like your present?"

"Who are you and what do want from me?" Ralph demanded.

The man on the other end laughed deep and hard. "You amuse me. Really you do. So, do you like how you look on camera? If you ask me you could stand to lose a few pounds." He laughed again.

Ralph closed his eyes and swallowed convulsively. "Can you please save all the small talk. How much do you want?"

"Did your wife watch it with you?"

"What?" Ralph queried, shaking his head. "What are you talking about?"

"The tape, Senator. Because if she didn't I have a few more she may enjoy." He snickered. "Remember, husbands and wives are supposed to share everything. I'm just helping you out. Surely she would want to know that her wonderful husband enjoys getting poked in the ass."

"Please . . ." Ralph began to tremble. "I'll do anything you ask. I'll pay you anything you want. Just don't, don't—"

"Change your Senate bid for David Huggins on Monday morning."

"Wha-what? This is about David Huggins? Did he put you up to this?" Ralph shouted. He cringed inside at the sound of the man's mocking laughter.

"I see you wanna play hardball," the man spat. His tone seemed to change drastically. "Fine. I have enough of your faggot, porno tapes to pass around to the whole Senate. Good day, Senator Carson."

"Wait!" Ralph shouted. His mind was spinning. He saw in vivid pictures what would happen. He and his family would be a laughing stock. His wife would leave him. Then he would be really destitute. Laura had the money. It was the only reason he had married her. She put up with a lot from him, but if she ever saw that tape his bank would be closed forever, and so would his life.

"I'll do whatever you want," Ralph finally whispered.

"Good. I knew you were a smart man. Now, this is what I want you to do . . ."

Kimberla was surprised to see Delphi already waiting for her in Central Park. She got closer to Delphi and could read the pain and stress on her face. When Delphi spotted her, she ran toward Kimberla with open arms.

"Girlfriend, you look bad!" Kimberla exclaimed. She pulled slightly away, looking Delphi up and down. There were more bruises and this time she hadn't attempted to conceal them with makeup. Her hair was ravaged. What usually was styled to the max and well kept was now a wind-tossed mess.

"You know you're gonna be okay. I'm just so glad you're out of that mess with Michael."

"So am I," Delphi whispered. She looked at Kimberla. "You said we needed to talk."

It was do or die. Kimberla knew she either had to take this gamble with Delphi, or risk wasting her chance and end up never finding out what truly happened to Margo. She choked back any reservations she had and began to speak.

"Delphi, were you serious when you said you were tempted to turn Michael in to the police?"

Delphi sat down on the wooden bench and casually threw rocks in the pond. She looked over at Kimberla suspiciously.

"You aren't going back to Michael with any of this, are you? After all, you do still work for him."

"Of course I won't!" Kimberla said indignantly.

"I'm serious, Alisha. He's had people killed for less." She closed her eyes and rubbed her crossed arms with both hands as if she were cold. "I'm sorry. I don't know who to trust."

Now was the time.

"Delphi, what would you say if I told you I don't really work for Michael?"

"What—what do you mean? Of course you work for him. You work for Mackings, you work for Michael."

"Okay." Kimberla took a deep breath.

"Come on, Alisha, what are you trying to say?"

Kimberla took a deep breath, and then the words spilled from her mouth. "My name is not Alisha; it's Kimberla. I'm not a dancer from Maryland. I'm a special agent from Washington, D.C."

No sound came from Delphi's mouth. She opened, closed, opened her mouth again, then suddenly started running. Kimberla immediately started after her.

"Delphi, wait!" she shouted.

Delphi tripped, drawing the attention of loads of park dwellers. Attention is the one thing Kimberla knew they didn't need. She closed in on Delphi, feeling more like a NFL football player than a sexy dancer.

"Wait, Delphi, please," she cried again as she grabbed one of her ankles. They both lay sprawled out on the sun-burned, spotty heaps of grass. "Give me time to explain."

Delphi was breathing heavy. Her face was twisted in fear. "I can't talk to you. I can't be seen with you. If Michael ever finds out about you I'm dead!"

"He's not going to find out." Kimberla grabbed Delphi by the arm. "And by the time he does, it's gonna be too late for him to do anything. Look," she said, sighing deeply, yet out of breath herself, "I'm sorry I deceived you. But at this point I need your help. You said you want to see Michael put away. This is your best opportunity to do just that."

"He . . . he killed that agent. That's why you're here, isn't it?" Delphi asked timidly.

"Yes it is. Can you tell me what you know about that?"

Delphi still didn't look convinced that she could trust Kimberla.

"What's gonna happen to me after you get Michael? I will still be jobless, and there will always be someone after me. Michael knows a lot of people."

"If Michael is responsible for as much as you say he is, you won't have to worry about him or anyone in his organization. It will be neutralized completely. I promise you, Delphi, we'll protect you. I need to know what happened to Margo Hunter."

"Who is Margo?"

"You said you knew about her. She is the agent we are talking about. And she was my very best friend," Kimberla stated sadly.

"When she was at Mackings she went by the name Carly Jennings."

"Okay, that's something I wasn't aware of. Do you know where she worked? Did she work for Mackings or for The Dorm or for both?"

"She was a hostess at The Dorm. I don't know that much about it though, Alisha," Delphi insisted.

"But you know people who do know, right? Will you help me, Delphi?"

Delphi didn't answer, but her eyes said yes. For the first time since coming to New York Kimberla felt she had gained ground. She knew she didn't have much time left, but maybe now with Delphi's help, she could find her way through the cracked door.

11

Brooklyn, New York

Michael Riley looked from Jacob to Mario Lincoln as he puffed away on his cigarette. There was a serious spirit emanating from him. Michael was usually the type of person that was always upbeat and calm. He waved his hand languidly at the door. Right away Mario jumped up and closed it; as a follower he always was there where Riley was concerned.

"I know you guys have been wondering about the plans," Michael said. "I have something big coming up and you will be in the forefront of it."

"You have been really quiet lately," Mario responded back. "I've thought maybe you had run into snags."

Michael laughed. "Do I look like the type of man who that would happen to? Listen up. We have four hundred kilos of pure cocaine coming our way. It will be flown in in just over a week. I need you two to widen our street market. Getting the product has been the main focus, but now that that's on schedule, we have to sell it."

Both Jacob and Mario were quiet, obviously for different reasons. Mario's face gleamed at the sum of cocaine Michael mentioned.

"Mike, do you know how much money that is on the street?" he asked with glee.

"That's just the beginning. We have a pipeline to get as much as we want, whenever we want."

"And what about getting through customs?" Jacob finally asked, coming out of his quiet shell.

He could feel the cracks in Michael Riley's concrete organization starting to open. For the past year since he had been undercover, Michael had been very cautious with him, only letting him in at small degrees.

"Brother, I've never had to worry about customs. Have you ever wondered why?"

"Yes, but I figured you would tell me when you were ready," Jacob replied.

Michael gave Jacob a sideways glance. "If you remember, Jonathon, I mentioned it to you before. I really didn't want to go deep into the plans until I was absolutely sure it was on schedule."

"So, tell us about it," Jacob said calmly.

Michael stood up and began walking around the room slowly. He turned his back slightly from Jacob and Mario, then swung back around, smiling broadly, as if he were about to announce the next president of the White House.

"You are right about the custom's rules, Jonathon. It would cost a quarter mil to earn a mil. And I don't like sharing money with those greedy sonuvabitches." Michael leaned on the chair that Jacob was sitting in then jumped up again, obviously feeling hyper.

"Calm down, Mike." Mario laughed. Michael laughed back.

His stalling was irritating Jacob. He knew he couldn't push him and make it seem too suspicious, but he could feel all the secrets he had been after for a year brimming on the edge waiting to be spilled over. He was about to just ask Michael straight out, till Mario beat him to the punch.

"So, who is your contact?" Mario queried.

"Someone you would never ever suspect," Michael said, grinning.

"You're taking a helluva long time to say it. Must be big," Jacob bluffed.

"David Huggins."

"Who the hell is that?" Mario asked.

Jacob didn't have to wonder, he knew exactly who it was. *Senator* David Huggins. The lead advocate in the New York Senate on tougher gun control and drug smuggling laws was in cohorts with one of the biggest drug kingpins in the country.

An hour after his meeting with Michael and Mario, Jacob made his way through the heavy Manhattan traffic to Kimberla's place. He wasn't sure why he was running to her. Laughing at himself he thought of the Whitney Houston song, "Run to You." What was it about this skinny, bossy, controlling sista that had him by the balls? He didn't know.

Jacob knew he wasn't going to tell her much about his meeting with Michael, so why was he so eager to see her?

Pulling the gears into park, he whispered to himself, "She's just a home reminder, that's all."

Jacob was thinking out loud, trying to convince himself of what, he wasn't sure, but it didn't slow his steps as he bounced his way up the stairs to Kimberla's apartment. He raised his hand to knock when the door suddenly came swinging open. There stood Kimberla and Delphi.

"Jonathon, um . . . hello," Delphi said in surprise.

"How are you, Delphi?" he asked. He looked toward Kimberla, who then reached out and squeezed Delphi's arm. Delphi seemed to be nervously avoiding his eyes.

"I'll see you later, girl. I'll call you, okay?"

"Okay," Delphi whispered. "What time?" Her eyes looked almost desperate.

"I'll call you later tonight," Kimberla responded. She reached out, giving Delphi another hug before Delphi quickly made her exit.

Kimberla took a deep breath then turned around to face Jacob.

"So, what's up?" he asked her.

Right away Jacob felt himself yanked by the shirt collar. "What, woman?" He laughed.

"What are you doing here?"

"I came to see you."

"Okay," Kimberla mumbled. She loosened her hold on his collar and sat on the edge of her couch. "As you saw, I had Delphi here. She's given me some very interesting info on Michael Riley."

Jacob was quiet for a moment, staring at her with warmth in his eyes. It seemed to make Kimberla blush.

"What's wrong?" Kimberla asked. "Why are you looking at me like that?"

"Spend the rest of the day with me . . ."

"Spend the day?" Kimberla asked in surprise.

"Yes." Jacob stood up, smiling softly at her. "Listen, I know that you haven't taken the time to do anything since you've been here but focus on this case. And to be honest, I haven't either. Let's see New York together." He reached out and touched Kimberla's cheek. "What do you say?"

"But don't you want me to tell you about Delphi? You told me to keep you updated on everything and I'm—"

"Shh . . ." he hushed her. "Is it going anywhere? Can't we just take a time-out? Spend the day with me."

"Spend the day. Like a date day? Are you serious?"

"Yes, I'm very serious. Come on, is the thought of a date with me so repulsive?" He laughed.

Flattery, surprise, excitement, and hesitation all merged together and coated her face. "I guess," she finally said.

"You guess?" He cocked his eye at her. "You guess the thought of a date with me is repulsive?"

"No, silly." She laughed. "I guess I will go out with you."

Women loved to play hard to get, he thought. He could see on Kimberla's face that she loved his idea, and could use some time out and relaxation. He resisted the urge to cock his head in victory and instead said, "I'll give you"—he looked down at his watch—"ten minutes to get ready." Her face lit up at his audacity. "What?" Jacob laughed.

"Okay, just let me change." As she started walking toward her bedroom Kimberla looked back at him, catching him giving her ass the eye. "And this is just touring the city, no funky business!"

"Of course," Jacob said. "Scout's honor." He saluted her. Funky business could have different definitions. He smiled at what that definition could be.

The evening went in a slow-moving daze for Kimberla and Jacob. The lights on Broadway sparkled in Kimberla's eyes, which Jacob seemed lost in. The two of them sat sipping on their drinks at the Kaplanlos's—a Greek restaurant famous for its flavored coffees. Jacob watched Kimberla's lips as she slowly licked the cream that had drizzled downward. He wondered if she was seeing anyone.

"Well, this has been interesting," she said quietly.

"What has?"

Kimberla waved her hands around her. "This—the whole New York thing. Definitely not the way I had planned to spend my vacation."

"And yet you insist on staying," Jacob stated with a smirk.

"Aren't you glad I did, since if I hadn't come you wouldn't be privileged to my wonderful company right now, would 'cha?"

Jacob's laugh filled the dining room, drawing the disturbed attention of all their fellow diners.

"You have this straight-up elevated opinion about yourself, don't 'cha?" he said with a smile.

"I'm a strong black woman, not some whimpering, whining chump." Kimberla batted her eyes.

"Okay, strong black woman, let's do something different."

"Like what?" Kimberla queried, wide eyed.

"We're touring." Jacob smiled. "We haven't seen anything yet. Come on, I have a surprise for you."

Jacob led the way and Kimberla followed as if walking on air.

12

Bronx, New York

Ronnie parked his car neatly in an alley lot behind "The Warehouse." The Warehouse was an urban, hip-hop gay club that was a hotspot for him. Good music, sexy chocolate men, and the best apple martinis in the Big Apple. It had been a long week for him. He was especially happy that his job with the greasy senator was over. Ronnie's stomach turned sour whenever he thought of the man's bloated, pig face. Getting out of his vehicle he shook the imagined wrinkles from his name-brand baggy jeans. He had decided to go urban, style wise, for the night.

"Ronnie, wassup, baby!"

Ronnie turned to the voice that was beckoning him. He smiled as he recognized Mao Washington, a sexy black dude with a brilliant smile.

"What's going on, sexy?" he cooed.

Mao raised his hand, giving him daps. "Where you been hidin'? You skippin' out on a brotha yo."

Ronnie opened the door to his BMW X5. His business had been good to him. "Why don't we skip into my buggy and I'll make it up to you," he said with a wink.

Mao quickly opened the passenger car door, slipped inside and relaxed back.

"So," Ronnie said as he slipped in beside him, "what's been going on?"

"Wait," Mao said suddenly, reacting to a strange noise on the outside of the car.

Ronnie jumped at a muffled pop sound. He looked at Mao to see if he had heard it, and fell back against his car seat as blood squirted all over him, blood that was fountaining from the caved hole in Mao's face. Flattening his body to the floor, Ronnie screamed as more gunshots flew through his BMW windows. He didn't know who the culprits were after—him or Mao—but with him being the only soul still breathing he knew that if he wanted to stay that way he had to get out of the car. He waited till the shooting quieted then opened the car door slowly, biting his lip in fear. He rolled out, hitting the ground, and heard a gruff voice say, "Where ya going?" He looked up at a pair of brown eyes and the long-nosed pistol that was pointed at him. The guy was after him!

"Ugg!" Ronnie cried out, pushing the guy back against his car. He ran, figuring if he could just get around the corner and out of the alleyway he would have a better chance. Running in a fast pace he gasped as he felt a hot burning pain in his left calf, piercing his muscles. He cried out again, this time in agony, but continued running with a hop.

"Where you going, faggot?" the guy said to him again.

A shot hit him in his left side. *Shit!* Ronnie thought, moaning, *I'm gonna die! I'm gonna die!* He fell face forward and started crawling as his blood poured out on the graveled dirt.

"Die, muthafucka!" the guy screamed out to him.

No! Ronnie thought. *I'm too young to go like this. I'm too—*

The man kicked him hard in his side where he had shot him, flipping him over. He was sudden face-to-face with his pursuer. A big black man with a gun pointed straight for his face.

"No, please don't!" Ronnie cried out, before being silenced by one shot, right between his light blue eyes.

*   *   *

An hour later an NYPD patrol unit pulled up in the alleyway behind the club.

A female officer paused briefly, noticing a body lying flat and immobile. She quickly buzzed her station, and said, "Possible 187. Officer in need of backup."

Getting out of her car, she walked over to the victim. Instantly she knew it was no longer a possibility. The young white male lying before her was definitely dead.

"Damn, woman, you got me dizzy!"

Kimberla laughed. Her eyes sparkled as the warm summer wind blew her short locks. They were at the top floor of the Empire State Building, standing at the glassy walls that surrounded them.

"Actually, I love high places," she said to Jacob. Her breath caught as he came behind her, wrapping his arms around her slim waist. A lover's embrace. Somehow it seemed so right, especially when Jacob ran his lips along the base of her neck.

"It's beautiful here, isn't it?" she whispered.

"You're beautiful . . ."

Beautiful? No one had ever used that word to describe her before. But if that's what Jacob thought, she wasn't going to complain. She turned to face him. Her eyes met his lips. What was so unusual to her and maybe one of the things she found most attractive about Jacob was his tallness. Most men couldn't challenge her much, height wise. But with him she felt not necessarily short, but feminine.

"What are we doing, Jacob?"

"Um . . . enjoying an evening together?"

"That's not what I meant." She laughed uncomfortably.

"Agent Bacon." Jacob lifted her chin, forcing her to look into his dark eyes. "Is there something wrong with letting go for an evening? With just being a woman? What's so weak about that?"

"I'm not saying it's weak."

"Then what's wrong?" he pressed. "I'm enjoying myself

with you. I've felt this chemistry between us ever since you came to New York, and I know you've felt it, too. Sometimes the job can become overwhelming. At least this one has for me. I'm still a man, Kimberla, and you are definitely a woman."

"What do you want to do?" she asked in barely a whisper.

He pressed her hips to his. "Let go. Just exhale for the night, and let go with me. Come home with me tonight."

Her breath caught and Kimberla didn't say a word. But she really didn't need to. The strong beat of her heart against his chest said it all.

Kimberla lay trembling, awaiting Jacob's return from the kitchen. She knew this was insane. She was always in control, although Jacob had no way of knowing how out of control she felt right now. When it came to sex it gave her great pleasure knowing she held the reins, and tightly. It gave her great pleasure knowing she could toy men around like puppets, making them dance to her song. Her body felt hot but still she pulled the silk sheets on Jacob's bed tighter beneath her chin.

He walked into his bedroom with an ice bucket, wine included, and two crystal tumblers in hand. His eyes bore into hers.

"Are you cold?" he asked, making himself comfortable on the edge of the circular bed.

"No, not really."

"Okay, then . . ." He pulled the sheets away from her. "Let me see. It's not like I haven't seen those beauties before." He winked.

"Negro, please." Kimberla rolled her eyes. She let the covers slip over her, determined to regain her control. She poked her breast out in a sexy pose, looking at him daringly.

Jacob swallowed. "Let's have some wine. Do you like Merlot?"

"I love Merlot."

While uncorking the wine, Jacob's hands shook. It comforted Kimberla to know she wasn't the only one caught up with nerves.

"What's wrong, Jonathon Simmons?" she teased, picking at his alias.

Jacob looked at her weakly. "I've never been too handy with these things."

"Well, I tell you what." Kimberla took the wine bucket and set it aside. "Why don't we forget about the wine right now. You may have seen my body before, but I haven't seen yours . . ."

She loosened his robe. It fell off his wide shoulders, providing a bird's-eye view of his sexy darkness. Jacob must have seen the awe in her eyes. He took the invite and moved over her quickly, covering her naked body with his.

"Mmm, Jacob," Kimberla moaned, feeling his largeness rubbing against the wet spot between her legs. She shivered again when his lips cascaded down her shoulders, to her chest. She let out a deep sigh as his lips covered one of her nipples and he began suckling her. Her breasts were extremely sensitive, and Jacob brought them alive.

"Oh yes!" she cried as he bit it softly, trying to slow her excitement. "Oh, God!" He licked down her rib cage to her flat stomach, sticking his tongue in and out of her navel. His lips went even lower, and she held her breath, waiting, waiting, till she felt his hot breath where she so needed it to be. Sticking his tongue out, Jacob licked around and around her swollen clitoris. Kimberla thrust her hips up to meet him.

"Yes, Jacob, yes . . ." she moaned. She looked down at his head that moved up and down in the same rhythm as his mouth and tongue. As she noted the waves of his hair, her body felt like them, as if she were floating on indescribable waves of pleasure. She put her hands on each side of his face and pressed. Her love juices poured from her, and he steadily sucked, licked, moaning against her as if he were eating a savory meal. Tingles made her thighs shake as Jacob paused, looking up at her. His lips were wet, coated with her arousal.

"Tell me what you want. You wanna come like this?"

"I don't—I don't know. I don't—"

Jacob smiled, and bent his head to her again, licking her from ass to clit, flicking his tongue rapidly at her button. Kimberla cried out.

"You wanna come in my mouth, baby?" he whispered to her again.

"I don't know, just do it! Please don't stop!" She pushed his head to her and thrust, and he went back to his feast, opening his mouth wide and devouring her, eating her, digging deep in the source of her pleasure. Kimberla felt her muscles tighten, her orgasm rising. She swung her head from side to side and moaned incoherently. She had never been taken to such oral heights.

Suddenly Jacob stopped.

"Noooo!" she cried out. "Please don't tease me, Jacob."

Her body shivered in pleasure, but she obviously wasn't the only one. Jacob flipped her over. He brought her to her knees and thrust hard inside of her, causing her to scream out again, almost falling from her kneed position. He pulled out, then thrust back inside, repeating the motion again and again and again.

"Damn," he heaved. "Damn . . ."

Kimberla could barely hear him. For the first time in her life, Chameleon, the strong black woman, lost control.

13

Brooklyn, New York

The sound of the alarm clock rang relentlessly in Jacob's ear. It shouldn't have been noise to him, but when someone is in a pleasure sleep, such as he was, any disturbance is noise.

He sat up stretching, then remembered Kimberla, and reached over to her. She wasn't there.

Hmm, he thought. Where was she?

"Kimberla?"

No answer. At first Jacob thought she was probably in the kitchen. After all the hot lovemaking the night before maybe she wanted to surprise him with her culinary magic. But then . . .

A tiny piece of paper caught his attention. Folded neatly and tucked under one of his cologne bottles. He picked it up and unfolded it.

Jacob, I don't really know what to say. I think both of us realize that last night was a mistake. I don't want anything to interfere in what we are trying to do here, meaning the case. I hope you aren't offended but please know it has

*nothing to do with you and everything to do with where I
am mentally right now.*

I'll talk to you tonight, at the club.

Kimberla

"A mistake, hmm . . ." Jacob voiced again out loud. Thinking
back to the night before, it had been anything but a mistake to
him. Maybe he had scared her, he wasn't sure. But Kimberla
wasn't the type of woman that could be scared away, or was
she?

Jacob sighed and flopped down on the edge of the bed, rubbing his temple in frustration. "Okay, maybe she wasn't feeling
it. No big deal. There are more fish in the sea," he said aloud to
himself. But in his mind he couldn't quiet the fact that there
were women everywhere, but very few like Kimberla Bacon. He
would have to call her and see what was up.

Just then the phone rang.

"Hello?" His heart hammered, hoping it was her.

"Jonathon." It was Michael Riley. "How soon can you get
to my office? There's someone here I want you to meet."

Looking at his watch Jacob replied, "I have to shower and
dress, but I guess I could get there in about hour."

"Make it forty-five," Michael stated, and hung up the phone.

Forty-six minutes later Jacob was knocking at Michael
Riley's door. He was secretly fuming inside that, for now at
least, he had to jump when Riley said jump. That would change
once he nailed him, for sure.

"Come in," he heard Michael demand. He walked inside
cautiously.

"You're a minute late, brother."

Jacob laughed. "Nigga, please. You counting seconds now?"
He eased onto the couch beside Michael's desk, this time happily excepting the mint offered. "So, what was the rushing me
over here about?" he asked.

Suddenly the office door opened, and in walked a very familiar figure.

"Senator, this is one of my trusted men, Jonathon Simmons. Jonathon, do I need to tell you who this is?" Michael asked with a sly smile.

Jacob was very aware of whom David Huggins was, but the question washing around in his mind was, what was a man like him doing chilling with Riley?

Huggins reached his hand out for Jacob's. "I hear you are a great one to have onboard. I hope you are also as trustworthy as Michael insists you are." His brow rose at his words.

"I'm loyal to those who are loyal to me," Jacob responded languidly. "So, what's going on here?" He looked from Michael to David Huggins.

"Nothing is wrong," Michael said. "You know I trust you, Jon. I trust you enough to introduce you to our forerunner." He looked at David Huggins. "I told you from the start that I had friends in high places, safeguarding our transport from various areas. Senator Huggins is seeking nomination for governor, as you may be aware, and in exchange for our help and support, he is supporting us, making sure we get our deliveries without interruption."

"Oh, I see," Jacob exclaimed as if impressed. His mind was working overtime. After a year he finally had what he was seeking: a name. But he needed more. He needed plans, dates, who, where, when. It took about twenty seconds for him to get just that.

Michael Riley reached across his desk to his gold cigar case, and took out three fat imports, handing one to each man.

That was one thing about this gig, Jacob thought, you get all the good things in life, while waiting to do away with scum like Riley. He took the cigar and smiled at both men.

David Huggins looked at Jacob pensively. "You do understand that we need the utmost discretion?"

Huggins looked like a comedian to Jacob. He spoke of discretion and yet he was lounging in the office of New York's finest. The finest, that is, in the category of pimp, drug smuggler, pusher, and murderer. Here he was with his bourgeois speeches about how he, if elected governor, would do away with the very things he endorsed.

Smiling at the joke of the politician, Jacob said, "My whole line of work is one of discretion, Senator. Don't worry, I'm the best man for this job. And Michael knows this. Don't you, Mike?" He looked toward Michael.

Michael laughed. "I sure do, brother." He addressed the senator again. "Don't worry, David, Jonathon likes to be a bit difficult at times, but he's a sure thing."

"Hmm . . . if you say so," David Huggins responded, still looking at Jacob cautiously.

"He knows so." Jacob nodded. "So, how do you plan on getting product through customs? I know, from what Michael has been going on about, we are talking massive here, not some small-change operation."

"Military aircraft never go through customs."

Jacob looked up at the senator in surprised. The look on his face made it pretty clear that he thought he had it all figured out. Maybe he did. No one would ever have figured out that system that was supposed to be used to protect was going to be used to bring in killer substances.

Fixing his face in a false glow of admiration, Jacob gave a mental toast of salute to Michael Riley and David Huggins, and winked.

She took a deep breath and counted backward from ten. She took another deep breath and still Kimberla seemed not to be able to still the nervous twitch that was rambling throughout her body. Her decision to leave before Jacob woke up was not an easy one. Never a woman to run from anything, she couldn't help but think that Jacob would read her actions as fear. Had she been afraid? Was she more afraid of Jacob or her own reaction to his lovemaking?

She brought her coffee cup to her lips; the liquid was cold, or maybe it was in comparison to the heat that was still residing within her. Cold and bitter. Not bitter at Jacob, though, more like self-embitterment. Oh gawd, she thought. Were her toes really still curled from the night before? Did he really turn her out that much?

She paused again, and then took a bite of her Sopressata and Swiss sandwich. She had skipped breakfast, but still at lunchtime she didn't feel that hungry. If things were different between Jacob and her, what would have happened? They would have slept till late morning; woken up wrapped in each others arms; greeted each other with a kiss, not even caring about morning breath. Embracing the day together in hot, heated lovemaking; losing themselves in each other's eyes; licking; tasting each other; rubbing and loving and—

"I'm losing my mind!" Kimberla screamed out loud. She was thinking like some overly romantic soap opera addict. She never had been one of those silly women sitting around waiting for Prince Charming to come and take her way. "Men have their purpose, and Jacob served his last night." She nodded her head, agreeing with her vocal announcement, then stood up, grabbing her still uneaten sandwich and cold coffee. "Yes, he definitely served his last night. But now I have better things to do."

The phone rang. Already standing, Kimberla rushed to pick up the receiver. "Hello?"

"Kimberla? It's Delphi."

"What's up, girl? Are you okay?"

Delphi sighed as if tired. "Yeah, but listen, I heard something about your friend, the agent?"

Kimberla swallowed hard. "Where can we meet?"

"I'm at Jobo's, on Park."

The sound of traffic blocked out the fear in Delphi's voice, almost. Her eyes were slightly red; her nose a bit puffy as she blew it once more.

"What did you hear?" Kimberla asked her once she seemed more composed.

"You won't believe this. I could hardly believe it myself. I mean I knew how ruthless Michael was but I had no idea that he could stoop to such lows . . ."

Kimberla swallowed. Delphi was making her nervous. "Why don't you just take a deep breath and tell me."

"Okay. I-I went to Mackings to pick up my last check. At least that's what my intentions were. Michael wasn't in his office so I decided to go in and see if any of the girls were on stage practicing." Delphi caught her breath. "I know this will sound bad, but I saw a friend of mine, a male friend. We used to be . . . you know, *intimate*." She looked at Kimberla for a reaction and when she got none, she continued. "He was asking me when we could hook up again, and knowing that I am, or was, Michael's personal friend, he pulled me into a back room alone. We talked for a bit, and he told me something that really shocked me."

"What is it? Come on, tell me."

"He said he was leaving Mackings."

Kimberla shook her head impatiently. "Come on, Delphi, why would that be so shocking? Who exactly is he and what does he do for Michael?"

"Keith used to be a bouncer for the club. Now he does side jobs." She looked at Kimberla and bit her lip. "He takes care of people who Michael tells him to, if you know what I mean. Anyhow," Delphi continued with a sigh, "he told me that he understood why I had left Mackings. I guess he doesn't know I was fired. Alisha—I mean, Kimberla—he told me about Carly, the woman you call Margo?"

"What about her?" Kimberla could feel her throat tightening.

Their waitress brought their entrées over, silencing their exchange. Delphi smiled slightly with trembling lips as she was served her roast beef and red potatoes. Her reaction unnerved Kimberla even more.

"Thank you," she said in a rush, addressing the slow-moving waitress. She gave her the eye to stop trying so hard to earn a tip.

Delphi covered Kimberla's hand with her own as the waitress walked away.

"Keith said he was there when Carly was brought to some warehouse. He said she was already dead. Shot in the head. But he said at the warehouse . . ." Delphi paused.

A knot seemed to cover the hole leading to Kimberla's wind-pipe, making her feel as if she was about to choke. She swallowed it. "Go on," she croaked.

"He told me how they got rid of her body, Kimberla. He said they cut her body up and cremated her. Burned her up in one of the old boiler rooms."

"What! Why? Why would they do something like that? She was already dead!" Kimberla almost shouted.

"They did it so no one would find her."

"Okay." Kimberla pulled one hand up, signaling Delphi that she needed to pause. "Okay, so why would Keith tell you about this?"

"He was warning me. You know Keith really hadn't been around much for the past month or so. He told me he's glad I'm not going to be working for Michael any longer, then he told me about Carly." Delphi paused, then grabbed Kimberla's hand, which was shaking. "I told you, Kimberla, Michael is a very wicked man. People say he had his own brother taken out. I'm not shocked that he would kill someone, have someone killed, but I am shocked that he would go to such extremes."

While quietly eating her food Kimberla mused over things. Her insides were shaking, but she didn't want Delphi to see that. She couldn't let anyone see how affected she was. *Oh, Margo,* she thought, *what horror you must have gone through.* Outwardly she said, looking at Delphi with steady eyes, "I'm going to kill Michael Riley."

14

Brooklyn, New York

Kimberla was late. Jacob had talked to her twenty minutes earlier and still no show. He couldn't help but think she was avoiding him. So many things were hopping around in his mind. David Huggins being the yank on the end of Michael's rope, his experience, and that was putting it mildly, with Kimberla, and the fact that she was late.

"Where the hell is she?" he exclaimed to himself. He took a big gulp of his cognac, letting the hot flavor of the liquor burn down his throat.

He couldn't help but think that he was getting a bit too anxious about Miss Chameleon. Hadn't she made it clear in her little note that what transpired between them was a mistake, and that she wasn't interested in taking it any further? Jacob wasn't the kind of man who had to beg a woman. What did he want to beg her for anyhow? What exactly did he want from her? Those were pertinent questions that he wasn't sure he was ready to answer. Not even to himself.

He jumped. The knock on the door caused his heart to start beating, fast. Putting his drink on the coffee table, he stood up and walked slowly to the door, then took a deep breath and opened it.

"Hi," Kimberla said, smiling at him nervously.

Jacob looked around her as if looking for someone.

"What, did someone keep you so busy or did you have trouble finding my place?"

"Don't start," Kimberla whispered. She pushed past him, walking into his apartment. "What was so important that you had to talk to me immediately? Have you found out anything?"

"Why did you leave?"

Stopping in midair, Kimberla was about to take a seat until Jacob brought up the dreaded question. He could see it on her face.

"Is that the reason you got me to come all the way over here?" Kimberla asked him with irritation.

"No, I wanted to talk to you about something else. But you know we have to talk. People just don't make love like we did then brush it off as 'oh, that was a mistake, my bad.' At least I don't."

She laughed. Jacob flushed inwardly, fighting hard to hide the raw embarrassment he felt from her diss.

"Forget it."

"No, no, I'm not laughing at you. I mean, I am." Kimberla giggled, still obviously unable to contain herself. "I'm not laughing at you for the reasons that you think. It's just that you are making it sound so serious as though just the other day you weren't making it hot and heavy with Lia Chamberlayne. Or was I walking into some private interrogation and just got the wrong impression?" She raised an eyebrow.

"Kimberla . . . are you really comparing the two?"

"I thought all men compared the women they slept with." She lowered her eyes.

"I don't. To me you and Lia are as different as a Bentley and a Kia Rio. Incomparable," Jacob said slowly, seductively. He could tell she was fighting hard not to blush, which seemed totally out of character for her. Blushing, that is. Deciding to take advantage of the situation, he reached over and caressed the nape of her neck with his fingertips. Kimberla shivered.

"I don't know if I like being compared to a car that you *ride*," Kimberla said, gasping once Jacob's limber fingers found their way down to her breast, squeezing one of her stiff nipples. "Jacob . . . oh!"

"You are no Lia Chamberlayne, Kimberla. Trust that."

"I don't trust her."

Diamond, the tall, slender girl standing next to Lia Chamberlayne, sighed in frustration, but kept quiet as Lia rambled on.

"I don't trust anybody who goes around thinking they are God's gift to the fuckin' world," Lia spat.

She hastily rubbed baby oil over her eyes, wiping away the residue of heavy eyeliner she had applied for her dance set.

"She ain't cute. I don't know why Michael even hired her ugly ass. All skinny and bony. Her black ass. She looks like a burnt-out match. Then she be on the stage doing that weird dance that's not even sexy. What's that called anyhow? What's that mess she be doing?"

"Delphi asked her once and she said it was called Kajukenbo. Some kind of martial arts thing. Actually I think it looks kinda cool."

"Cool?" Lia exclaimed, almost shouting. "It looks dumb. I wish she would try some karate crap on me. I'll stab her ass with a fork! She's trying to get her paws into Jonathon. I just know she is."

Lia brushed passed Diamond, knocking Diamond's purse off the makeup table, causing lipstick and eye shadow along with a wrapped tampon to scatter to the floor.

"Shit!" Diamond cried as she bent down in retrieval.

"Oops. Sorry. I'm just mad, girl." She bent down, helping Diamond pick up her things. "I'm gonna keep my eye on Alisha Howard. You just watch me."

"Goodness, Lia, I'm trying to go home and all you can do is sit around whining about Alisha!" Diamond rolled her eyes, sighing again.

Lia walked toward the door, completely ignoring Diamond.

"I'm gonna keep my eye on you, Alisha," she continued to mutter to herself. "Just watch."

Still in a fury, Lia walked hastily past Michael Riley's office, then paused. She pushed the door open and fixed a bright smile on her face.

"Hey, Michael."

"What the hell is wrong with you busting in here like that?" he said calmly. Michael was always calm, even when he was upset.

"I'm upset."

"You're upset?" Michael laughed. Pushing his chair back from his desk, he held his arms open to Lia. The slight irritation that was formerly in his voice had dissipated. Lia knew right away what was up. "Lock the door . . ." he whispered.

"Hmm . . ." Lia hummed. She walked over to his office door and closed it quietly. Looking back toward him, she licked her lips. "Michael, I really wanted to talk to you about Alisha."

Arms held open wide, Michael seemed to be ignoring her. She walked slowly into them, sighing in frustration as he wrapped her up. He squeezed her slightly and moved his hands down to her thin cotton dress, then he cupped her ass tightly.

"You gonna give me some of this?" he asked, pushing her back against his desk.

"I want—I want to ask you about Alisha. I want to talk to you. I think there's something fishy about her."

Michael slipped his fingers inside Lia's panties, rubbing downward toward the apex of her sex.

"Michael, please," she crooned.

"We can talk about Alisha after we talk about this."

He stuck two fingers deep inside her. Hearing her gasp of pleasure, he smiled.

There was a burning sensation. What should have been painful was instead searing, breathtaking pleasure. Jacob was branding her with hot wax that dripped down the concave of her spine. He branded her with the feel of his tongue that followed the dripping wax.

"You're addictive, Kimberla Bacon," he whispered, kissing her back again. He caught his breath. "Addictive."

Kimberla sighed inwardly. She hoped her face didn't reflect just how good he had made her feel. Although from the screams and moans she'd heard coming from her mouth, there was no doubt he already knew.

"You amaze me," Jacob said. He put the lit candle on the end table, and pulled her into his arms. He kissed her forehead tenderly. He was tender and romantic—qualities that were so new to Kimberla but that Jacob held in spades.

"How do I amaze you?"

"Just the way you hide how you feel. No one would ever guess . . ."

"Guess what?"

"That you are just as warm and tantalizing inside, as you are controlling and demanding outside. That is all a front." Jacob smiled. He knew that would get a rise out of her. And it did.

Kimberla sat up; her eyes were smarting but she was still unable to hide the slight smile on her face. "I am not controlling, thank you!"

"But you are beautiful . . ."

"Thank you."

Even though her eyes were averted, Kimberla could still feel Jacob's eyes burning into her skin. They had just finished . . . doing what? Making love? She would like to consider it having sex, but the glow of joy she felt radiating throughout her body somehow made her know that was deleting the worth of what had happened. Still, the next words that came from Jacob's mouth shocked her.

"What would happen if we fell in love, Kimberla?"

"What! Why would you say something dumb like that?" she stormed.

Jacob sat up abruptly. Then looked at Kimberla. "I was kidding, you know? Why you tripping?" He laughed.

"I'm not tripping," Kimberla whispered as she got up from the bed and started walking toward the bathroom. She jumped as Jacob made his way behind her, wrapping her in his arms from behind. He kissed her neck.

"Look, I really was kidding. But is love such a bad word to you?"

"I just don't feel it should be thrown around lightly," she breathed. Allowing Jacob to turn her around so she could face him, Kimberla's eyes barely met his.

Why he was playing this game with her was beyond the reasoning of Kimberla's mind. Men played games, always had, always would. That was one of the reasons to only keep them for the purpose they were intended for. But even though she tried to convince herself that this was what she felt and needed from Jacob, her heart would not stop its quick beating.

"You are right," Jacob finally said to her, after a minute of intense staring. "So now that you've gotten me straight, how about you rejoin me in my bed, or I can join you in the shower, hmm?"

With a laugh, Kimberla gently pulled him along with her, to get wet.

15

East Manhattan, New York

While driving the short distance to pick Lia up for the club, Jacob's mind was playing all kinds of tricks on him. He couldn't help but wonder if he had actually played himself. She was feeling the sex, no doubt. But anything outside of that? Jacob's face, as dark as it was, almost reddened in remembrance of his so-called joking words and Kimberla's reaction. It had been so long since he had felt anything for a woman. So even as much as he considered himself to be a lighthearted playboy, with Kimberla, he didn't know what to say. He was more serious than he was letting on. He wanted more from this woman; he wanted to delve deeper into her thoughts, her feelings. After the orgasmic sparks dissipated he didn't feel the same as he usually felt with other women such as, well, Lia Chamberlayne. Let's face it, a hot piece of ass was a hot piece of ass. But Kimberla, she was so much more. But there was something holding her back, something that was making her keep him at arm's length. At least emotionally she was. Jacob's mind kept racing over the time they spent together. His ears kept hearing the words she'd said; the words he'd said; sparks that were felt from them both. Maybe she couldn't see him as anything but a sex mate because that was all, at this time, that they had done together. Maybe it was time he changed his game plan.

He pulled up at Lia's high-rise apartment building. It took one minute for her to come bouncing out the front doors with a full smile coating her face.

"Well, you're on time," she cooed after closing the passenger door. She reached over and gave him a quick kiss on the cheek.

"It's not like I'm usually late."

"Well no, but you have been rather ignoring me lately."

Jacob looked to his left, witnessing her pouting expression, and couldn't stop the laugh that sprung out of his mouth. This chick was a trip, he thought.

"And what's so funny?" Lia spat. "You know I haven't heard from you in days, Jon-Jon. What have you been into, or rather," she raised one eyebrow, "*who* have you been into?"

Swallowing the touch of irritation that began to rise, Jacob was quiet for a minute. It killed him how Lia, a woman who he knew for a fact was fucking half the men that worked for Michael, could take it on herself to question what he did, and who he did it with. After his moment of silence he decided to ask her just that.

"Who has been your latest bedmate, Lia? Do you see me telescoping who you are fucking?"

"Hmph," she grunted.

"Hmph is right. I don't ask your business, you don't need to know mine. I'm just doing you a favor by picking you up for work so your ass wouldn't have to take a cab. So don't be trippin'."

"Jonathon, you never used to talk to me like this. I think you've been spending too much time with that hoe-ass, Alisha. I don't trust her, and you shouldn't either!"

"And why don't you trust her?"

Lia laughed. "Other than the fact that she looks like a man? Shit, she could be a transsexual or something. But other than that, it's because we don't know a damn thing about her. And you best be careful, too, or folks may start to think you like little boys."

"Well, if that's true you'd best be careful yourself. The way you been sniffing my jock, folks may start to think you're a fag hag who likes homos." Jacob laughed.

"That's real cute, Jon-Jon."

"Thank you," Jacob responded, smiling as they pulled up to Mackings' entrance. "Here we are. I guess I'll talk to you later, baby."

Lia gave him a questioning look. "Aren't you staying for the show tonight?"

"No, I have some business to take care of in Crown Heights. I'm sure you can catch a ride home from someone else."

"Fine." Lia was obviously still riled with him. "I need to talk to Michael again anyhow. About that she-male."

Jacob grabbed her arm just as Lia was about to step out of his SUV. "What is your obsession with Alisha? What do you have to talk to Michael about her for?"

"I don't trust her. I told her that!" Lia yanked her arm away. "Shit, as far as we know that bitch could be five-O. And there you are, sleeping with the enemy. Just keep on getting your groove, Jonathon, but I'm gonna find out just who the fuck she is."

The small dressing room that all her dancing sisters shared seemed extra-crowded this night. The noise sounded extra-loud. Kimberla knew it was probably because her mind was so busy. Here she was in New York City and her objective had been to find out what had happened to her best friend and com-rade. Instead she was getting deeper and deeper involved with a past crush and a fellow agent, and that was not good.

She slipped on the satin black panties that were going to shield her unmentionables tonight. She was wearing a black, see-through mesh miniskirt, and a black, lace, underwire push-up bra. She took her hair wrap off and swung her hair loose, then used a soft brush so that it would be bouncing and behav-ing. Noticing the slightly red passion mark that was on her neck, her thoughts went back to Jacob. She wondered if he was thinking about her right now. Not that she wanted him to.

"Alisha, you're on next," the soft-spoken Diamond, one of Michael's top dancers, called out from the door.

Okay, here we go again, Kimberla thought to herself. She took a deep breath and headed for the doorway. As she passed through she bumped head on into Lia Chamberlayne. Lia jerked back as if she had been burned. Kimberla looked at her sour expression and shook her head.

She was beginning to become a pain.

She lost herself in the music. At this moment it wasn't about the investigation; it wasn't about stripping or getting information on Margo's killers. It was about the music, something that had always touched her soul. This time there was something different about her dance. Kimberla felt more sexual, more beautiful, and more alive. And her thoughts were on one man. Jacob White. She danced for him, even though he wasn't in the audience. Here she could let go and express the feelings she felt inside, ones she hadn't even acknowledged to herself.

As she clung to the long dancing pole, in her mind she was clinging to Jacob. His comment when they had last been together, asking what if they fell in love, burned in her memory. What if they did? Kimberla wondered if she'd even know love if it hit her square in the face. For some reason she wanted to know more about him, Jacob, the man. This was a first for her, as if the crush she had in college never truly went away.

Her body became hot as her dance drew to an end. Her mesh skirt was off, and when the last melody flowed, off came her lace bra. She smiled at the oohs and ahs in the audience and made her way offstage.

From the corner of her eye she saw a familiar face: a short white man with a bad haircut. Malcolm Johnson. Their eyes met for a long minute and she felt the enraptured feelings and thoughts about Jacob that were present during her dance evaporate.

She would find out why he was here later, but she couldn't give him too much attention, not *here*. She turned away and again attempted to make her way offstage to the dressing room when she realized that another pair of eyes were on her: the suspicious ones of Lia Chamberlayne. She had watched the visual exchange between Kimberla and Malcolm Johnson.

"Who's the white guy?" Lia snarled at her as she passed. "A fan?"

"I guess so," Kimberla answered back. "He wouldn't be the first one, would he?"

"Nope. You know white men do love skinny dark girls like you."

Kimberla ignored that stupid comment, but her fist was itching to land somewhere. She kept walking to the dressing room until she could not longer smell Lia, the heffa.

The night had been too long. With the mixture of having to deal with Lia and then Malcolm showing his ugly face, Kimberla felt exhausted. She held her vinyl tote close to her. After all, this was New York. It was absolutely nothing for a street bum to come along and try to mug her, and she would hate to have to whip some poor kid's ass tonight.

She wondered where Jacob was.

Her mind was playing tricks on her. She just couldn't get that sexy-ass man out of her thoughts. Kimberla shook her head as if that would help, then raised her hand in an attempt to hail a cab. A car pulled up and the passenger-side automatic window rolled down. Malcolm Johnson was grinning through it. Kimberla let out a sigh as he nodded for her to get in, opening the door as he did so.

Sitting down but not too comfortably, she waited for him to speak.

"Wow . . . wouldn't Kyte Williams be shocked if he saw what his favorite agent was up to," he said with a smirk.

Kimberla hid a grimace. "Whatever. What are you doing here? I thought Micah Latimer was supposed to be checking up on the case?"

"Latimer had a death in the family. So I decided to come see what you were up to myself. And . . ." he eyed her provocatively, ". . . it seems you're up to quite a lot."

"I'm undercover. Don't show what a snake you really are, Malcolm. I would crush your little head under my heel."

Malcolm laughed out loud. "Okay, Wonder Woman. What have you found out about Margo?"

"This is not a good place to talk about it." Kimberla stirred uncomfortably.

"Then where do you live? We can go there right now."

"Like hell!" she stormed. "I don't want you near my place. I'll meet you in the morning and we can talk about it over brunch."

"What's happened to her, Kim? Don't play games with me. You're in enough trouble as it is!"

"Who the fuck are you screaming at?" Kimberla shouted back. "I hope you know that regardless of who you think you are I still outrank your ass!"

"And I hope you know, outside of that humongous ego of yours, that this case isn't about rank, it's about Agent Hunter. Or have you forgotten about her?"

Now that was hitting below the belt, and it brought tears to Kimberla's eyes. This was all about Margo. From the very start it had been about her. But Malcolm brought out Kimberla's worst qualities. He was not the first to say she had an oversized ego though. Sebastian Rogers, who had been one of her ASAICs, always said the same thing about her, so she'd heard on the low. Funny thing about Sebastian was that it was he who had the oversized ego. And that inflation had destroyed him. She was so sick and tired of men who felt threatened by her position.

"No," Kimberla said through clenched teeth, "I have not forgotten about Margo. It's odd, Malcolm, you never seemed to like Margo before and now you are so overly concerned with this case. Or could it be that you became concerned once you found out that I was in New York, looking into things?"

"I'm here because I was sent by Kyte. If you have a problem with that, you would best address that to him."

Malcolm paused for a moment and popped an old AC/DC cassette in his stereo system. That irritated her, too.

"How about we start over," he suggested. "Why don't you let me take you home, and we can talk again tomorrow?"

Ignoring his suggestion, Kimberla decided she would much rather take her chances with a cab then spend another second in his presence.

She stepped out of his car and was about to close the door when she heard him call out to her again. It made her heart beat extremely fast, because she wasn't the only one who heard him call out the name, Kimberla.

Lia Chamberlayne was standing almost beside the car, and her eyes shot daggers.

16

Brooklyn, New York

The entire night was rather slow. The stars that had danced over Jacob's head seemed to retire. In its place was an orange-like glow letting New Yorkers know that a new day was rising.

He had spent the night with Mario Lincoln collecting product funds. As always, Mario was vicious when it came to dealing with their street vendors. Earlier in the night he had been extra vicious. They broke into Drone Maxwell's crib unannounced. Drone was the type of kat that used his money for foolishness. Foolishness being, he threw the money on hookers when the fact was he didn't need to spend money, he could usually get it handed to him for free. The problem was Drone seemed to be throwing away money lately, yet he was coming up short in his hustle. Mario wasn't having that.

"I'm telling you, Mario," Drone had said in a voice shaking with nervousness, "I don't know wassup with these young kats who be rollin' wit' me. They say sales just ain't as good as they were before, yo."

"Is that so?" Mario had looked at Drone in amusement, although Jacob knew he wasn't laughing. "So is that what you want me to tell Mike?" He stuck a loaded .38 at Drone's temple. "Or would you like to take a ride and you can tell him yourself?"

Drone's face was devoid of color. Everyone knew that Mike didn't play, not when it came to his money or his product. Cross him and you may just end up six feet under.

The temperament in the room seemed to get very tense. It was such moments when Jacob worried about his cover, and how or when enough was enough. Mario hadn't been with the organization long, but Jacob could tell by the violent actions he resorted to that if things didn't come to a head soon, it wouldn't be long before he would kill. Jacob had even himself managed to resort to petty violence so as not to appear soft. Sometimes he worried that Mario would question the way he interacted with their street hounds. So there was a fine line he couldn't cross, one of violence, that is, yet at the same time he had to maintain a sense of toughness to carry on his cover.

Eventually they left Drone's apartment when he managed to remember the extra stash of cash he had that belonged to Michael. Lucky for him, his head was still attached to his body. But Mario had said he would put a birdie in Mike's ear that Drone was not to be trusted, which was death to any street hustler. If your word wasn't bond in the streets, very few people wanted to deal with you.

Shaking himself from his backtrack daydream of the night's activities, Jacob threw water on his face, then looked in the mirror. He was tired. This case was taking too long. He knew when he got involved that it would be long and tiresome, but for some reason ever since Kimberla had been in the picture he was eager for it all to be over and done with. What the future would hold for him and her, he had no idea, but he definitely wanted to explore the possibilities. The problem was she didn't seem to feel the same way.

The phone rang, surprising Jacob. He was surprised also when he looked at the clock and saw that he had spent the past two hours dreaming backward over the night's happenings and hadn't been to bed yet. He picked up the receiver.

"Hello?"

"Well hello, sexy," a soft familiar voice sang.

"What the hell? Hennessy Lewis!" Jacob heard her soft laugh and immediately felt a warmth come over him.

"No, Hennessy Jackson now. Tristan and I were married two months ago, you know."

"Well congratulations. I think."

Hennessy laughed again. "Okay, I know everyone is still a bit disconcerted about my choice but I am extremely happy, Jacob."

Jacob laid his head back against the bedpost, smirking slightly at Hennessy's words. She and he used to be rolling partners back in the day. Their D.C. days. After the L.A. events as weird and wild as they were, and her leaving the agency and hooking up with Tristan Jackson, a notorious, or, as she liked to say, ex-notorious criminal and jewel thief, the two of them had lost touch. It was great hearing from her again.

"Your being happy is my only concern, Hennessy. You know that. But tell me, what are you doing in New York? I didn't think anything could pull you away from New Mexico."

"Well you know I come home once in a while to see my parents. Tristan was going to come with me but he had a lot to do at the ranch. We got a few mares that we have been getting ready to race in England. He's trying to get them trained and all now, so I decided to come see my parents before that."

"Good, good. So how did you know where to find me?"

"Why would you ask me something like that?" Hennessy responded. Jacob could almost see her dimpled grin. She was in good spirits. He supposed Jackson did that for her. If it were possible to see a woman sparkle through the telephone, she was shining like a new penny. "I always keep up with you. You know this."

"I'm glad somebody cares . . ."

"Hmm. Do I sense some ambivalence in your tone? What's wrong, darling?"

"Other than I need a vacation?" Jacob answered back. "I'm okay." He glanced over into his dresser mirror, noting the tiredness on his face.

"I won't ask you about what you are up to right now, work-wise. Or can I?" Hennessy asked in a whisper.

"Hennessy . . ." Jacob warned.

"Okay, okay. I'm just joking." She laughed. "But listen, if you ever need to talk, off the record, you know I'm good for it all right?" She paused for a moment. "Is it a woman problem?"

Jacob laughed. "You don't give up, do you?"

"Okay, secret papi, just call me whenever!"

"I will."

"I mean it," Hennessy said with a chuckle.

"Hey, I don't have your new number."

"My cell number is the same. Night, darling."

After three hours passed by, Jacob finally managed to get some much-needed sleep. He was right in the middle of a hot dream of Kimberla. He'd just finish sucking her toes and was moving sensuously up her ankles to behind her knees, planting wet licks as he went, when the telephone's chime woke him up.

"Shit!" he exclaimed as his eyes popped open. He felt around for the phone, feeling frustrated and hard. There were two things you didn't mess with when it came to him. His Ice House beers and his wet dreams.

"Who is it!" he screamed into the receiver.

"Jon-Jon, I need to talk to you." It was Lia.

"Lia, damn. I've been up and out all night long and haven't that long ago gotten to sleep. Can't this wait? If you need a ride to Mackings later, fine. I'll call you back tonight."

"No, it's not about that. Although I do need a ride. It's about your friend, Alisha or Kimberla, or whatever that bitch's name is."

That woke him up.

"What are you talking about? Why are you calling Alisha Kimberla?" Unbeknownst to Lia, Jacob's heart was beating fast and his mouth was as dry as sandpaper as he asked her this.

"Well your girl had some white man trying to holla at her at the club last night. She even got in his car. I was outside trying to find out where her nasty ass had gone off to and I saw her get out of his ride. He called her 'Kimberla.' He knew her, Jonathon. I keep telling y'all something ain't right with that bitch. And this just goes to prove *me* right."

Sighing inside, Jacob whispered, "Maybe that's just a pet name for her or something. You know how those customers can get. They sometimes make up all kinds of fantasies. Lia, I think you're putting far too much energy into Alisha. You're too smart and beautiful a woman for that."

He hoped his flattery would get her mind on something else. But he was damning Kimberla all over the place for getting so sloppy around Lia! As intelligent an agent as she was, sloppiness was out of character for her.

"There you go, still defending her," Lia said accusingly. "She could be fucking the white man. And she's supposed to be with you? I would think you'd be pissed about this, Jonathon."

"Who says she's supposed to be with me?"

Lia laughed. "Oh come on now. You think everyone is not talking about what a hot pair you two are? You just kicked me to the curve for that hoe and now she's either fucking some white dog or she's an imposter. I tend to think both are true!"

"Listen . . ." Jacob sighed again, then ran his hands over his tired eyes. "I need to think about all this. I'm also going to ask Alisha about it. Just do me a favor and keep it to yourself for now, okay?"

"Why?"

"Because I'm asking you to. I'll talk to her myself and see wassup with that."

"And why shouldn't I tell Michael?"

"Because goddamn it, I asked you not to! You're right about one thing. She and I are seeing each other. I wanna find out what the fuck is going on. This is personal, Lia."

"Okay, don't scream at me. It's not my fault that she's—"

"I have to go," he broke in. "I'll talk to you later." Jacob hung up the phone.

Actually he was upset. Not for the reasons that Lia thought. He had to find a way to make Kimberla leave New York, immediately. He jumped up from his bed. His sleep had been disrupted enough that it didn't matter anymore. At this point he just needed to talk to her.

Thirty minutes later he was knocking on Kimberla's door; she opened it and smiled a welcome at him.

"Hey, I was just about to call you."

"I've had enough calls for the morning, thank you," Jacob said as he walked hurriedly inside.

"Hmph. Who stuck a stick up your ass this morning? Or did you just wake up on the wrong side of the bed?"

He watched as Kimberla's hips swayed from side to side as she walked over to pour herself a cup of coffee. Even though he was pissed at her, his body always seemed to react to her presence.

"Kimberla, why didn't you call me right away last night after what happened with Lia?"

"What do you mean?" she asked evasively.

"You know what I mean! Who was the white guy you got in the car with? What have you been up to? You realize that Lia heard him call you Kimberla? Do you realize it's over? You have to get out of New York. I mean that!"

"She didn't waste a moment calling you, did she?"

Jacob walked over to her, turning her face to force her to look at him. "Who was he?"

"Jacob, you're acting like you really are my man or something. And that you're jealous." She laughed. He did not. He was jealous.

"Who was he?"

"Lawd. It was Malcolm Johnson. You said yourself that headquarters would soon send someone else to find out what happened to Margo, and you were right." Kimberla looked up at him defiantly. "Happy now?"

Jacob walked up closer to her. Licked his lips, closed his eyes, then opened them again to see her staring into his. "You know I really don't want you to go. But you have to," he said somberly. "I'm just worried, Kim. And it's not just because of you possibly blowing my cover."

"What else are you worried about?"

His face took on a pained expression. Jacob hadn't felt emotions this strong for any woman since his wife. But he couldn't tell Kimberla that. Every feeling he showed her other than sexual ones seemed to scare her to death.

"You have this 'you can do it all yourself' attitude, Kimberla. This time you can't. And I know these kats we're dealing with. I know Michael Riley and I know what he's capable of. For now I'm able to control Lia a bit but I don't know how long I'll be able to hold on to that and keep her from going to Mike with her suspicions. I'm also concerned about how emotionally involved you are with everything. You are not the right agent to be on this case. You and Margo were too close and you know it. I can't even at this point figure out what you are trying to do."

"I just need to know everything, for my own peace of mind. I need to know that Michael gets what he has coming to him!"

"I really care about you . . ." Jacob said softly, as if he was in his own world. His eyes never left hers.

"Why are you saying this? You switch up on me so much, Jacob, I'm starting to think you're bipolar. Besides, don't be trying to get all luvvy-luvvy with me. You know your care and concern is your cover or whatever you're trying to do. All the secrets that you don't trust me with."

"I care about you, Kimberla," he repeated, "and I'm worried about you. I know you have to see that my biggest concern is your safety, not just my cover. But you're professional enough to know that's a concern, too. And don't be trying to change the subject." He lifted her chin, forcing her eyes to look into his again. "You know what I'm feeling for you."

"You're all over the place. I'm not sure what we're even talking about here," she said breathlessly.

Jacob didn't say any more words, he simply caught her last ones in his mouth with a deeply penetrating kiss.

17

New York City

She was starting to get confused. No, she was confused. Kimberla's thoughts kept flexing from Jacob, Margo, Lia to Michael, then to Malcolm. She wasn't even sure why she was staying in New York at this point, or what she hoped to accomplish now that Malcolm was on the case and Jacob seemed unwilling to let her in on what he was actually doing. Maybe she was risking her career for nothing. Maybe she should just fly to Maryland and spend the much-needed time she had promised to her father and stepmother.

Her state of mind was starting to get to her. Mental level-headedness had always been her strong point and it seemed to be evaporating quickly, leaving her in a mind mess that needed to be cleared up. Her racing thoughts gained speed after Jacob left. Kimberla's position was clear in her head. Her thoughts only became jumbled when Jacob questioned her.

She wanted to be the one to get evidence on Michael; she wanted to be the one to nail him. That was the problem.

What she needed to do was stop fantasizing about Jacob and start conducting herself like the agent in charge she was. He was right, she was getting sloppy. The mishap with Lia was so unlike her. Working undercover had always been her specialty. Shit, she had trained more agents than she could count—trained them how to be smart, convincing, but most of all, safe. And look at her now.

It was Jacob's fault. It was the sex. The sex had made her weak, like kryptonite, she thought with a laugh.

All these thoughts mulled around in her head while she was in the taxi on the way to Mackings. It was later in the evening, and she didn't have to dance that night. But she still needed to be at Mackings. She had something better in mind. She rubbed her hand over the small lump in her purse as her cab pulled up to the club. She wondered how she could get into Michael's office, plant her bugging device on his phone, and get out again without anyone noticing her.

"Here you are, Chameleon," the cab driver said to her.

Kimberla looked at him questioningly.

"I've seen you dance. And I must say, pretty lady, you are hot!"

"Thanks." Kimberla laughed. She handed the cabby a fresh twenty. He handed it back to her.

"No, this ride's on me. It's my pleasure."

"Are you sure?"

"Very. I tell you I'm a big fan!" The man was beaming.

Uh-huh, Kimberla thought. She could see the lust in his eyes. Men were all the same; they never changed. She laughed at her hypocrisy while smiling back at his big fat grin. She supposed that with women around taking off their clothes and licking their hard nipples onstage—the part she was playing, of course—the little puppy men had no choice.

Surprisingly, Jones was not at the door with his ever-goofy smile, looking for a way to get on her nerves.

She walked freely through the heavy doors. The hallway was empty. Kimberla couldn't help but think that God was with her somehow, even if God had nothing to do with this. But then she had picked this time of the evening because she knew everyone's routine. Michael usually wouldn't come in till after seven, and the club didn't get to rolling till after nine or sometimes as late as ten. Anyone who would be practicing was in the dressing rooms or onstage. So the only person she'd been concerned about was Jones, and with him out of the way . . .

Just to be safe, she called out his name.

"Jones! Where are you? Is anyone here?"

Silence.

Sighing in relief, she walked farther down the hallway to Michael's door. She looked around one last time for good measure. When she opened the door, it made a soft, creaking sound. She stopped suddenly when she heard a deep, feminine moan. *Oh just great!* she thought. She backed away from the door and followed the sound. To the right of Michael's office was a small utility room. The moans seemed to be coming from that direction. Kimberla cracked the door open slightly so as to go unnoticed.

There was Jones, buried mouth first and head second between the quivering legs of Heaven, and he was licking away. Heaven was one of the Mackings dancers who usually danced earlier in the night. That meant she was considered of lesser quality to pull the men and the money in for the club. She had her eyes sealed shut and was jerking her hips up and down and pressing Jones's head deeper into her privates, while grinding against his mouth.

"Ooooohhhh," she cried. "Ooooohhh!" She moaned like a cat in heat.

The whole sordid scene had Kimberla's stomach on the verge of regurgitating. She crept quietly away from the door, and shut it.

"Now that's nasty," she whispered to herself.

But as nasty as it might have been, their sexual business gave her time to take care of her own business.

Minutes later she was finally back in Michael's office. It took her mere seconds to get the bug placed inside his desk phone receiver. What was she looking for? She was hoping to hear or find out anything; any clue as to the real culprits who had killed Margo. But mostly she needed to know why Margo was killed.

"There," Kimberla said, taking a deep breath as she closed the office door.

Now she needed to go to the dressing room and act like she was at the club for legitimate reasons. God only knows who had seen her walk through the main door. She had to have a good excuse.

Once she was in the changing room she unlocked her locker and started fiddling with the clothes she had left in there, trying to figure out which were in need of laundering.

"What are you doing here?" a voice called from behind her.

She turned around and, to her surprise, it was Michael Riley. She jumped.

"Damn, you scared me to death!"

"Well, you shouldn't be so nervous. I won't bite you." He smiled at her. The man had too much charm. But she always knew from her dealings with those foul creatures called men that charm was as deceptive as the devil. Michael seemed always to go out of his way to appear to be the sweetest thing on earth.

She forced a laugh. "You're just so handsome I can't help myself," she teased.

Michael's eyes lit up, and Kimberla wanted to kick herself. The last thing she needed was to have this fool thinking she was interested in him. He had enough of the girls sniffing his jock, and her nerves were the reason for the slip of the tongue.

"Why, Alisha," he said smugly, "I didn't think you noticed. One would think you only have eyes for my brotha Jonathon." He walked up close to her and ran his hand tenderly across her cheek. "You know I was a bit jealous at first."

"Jealous of what?" Kimberla croaked. She was fighting to swallow the bile that had gathered in her throat from his touch.

"Of the fact that I saw you first, yet Jon is the one enjoying the pleasure of this . . ." Michael paused in midsentence. The hand that had caressed her cheek was now cupping her behind. ". . . this sexy, sexy ass."

Although she wanted to push him away and kick *his* ass, a smart agent knew when to play along in a sticky situation. She held back the strong urge to break a few of his fingers and have him sprawled on his back from a fresh Kajukenbo move. The thought of such violence against him made her smile. She pulled away slightly.

"Michael, Jonathon and I are just doing what the younger folks would call chillin'." She tried to laugh.

"Chillin' how? What kind of things do you do for him? Do you give him head? Do you wrap those long, sexy legs around him the way you do that pole on stage?"

Michael's words seemed to excite him more and more. Kimberla could feel him getting hard against her stomach. It was time to put a proper end to this madness.

"Michael, I really have to go. I just came in to get my dirty dancewear..."

"Does he eat you out?" he asked heatedly, vulgarly.

She was getting pissed. Her thoughts about how men really were, even those who pretended to be charming, had just been validated.

She supposed her feelings registered on her face, because Michael laughed heartily and smacked her ass.

"I was just joking with you, sista."

Kimberla tried to laugh with him. She was more relieved that he had finally removed his hand though.

"You so crazy," she said with a nervous giggle. She reached up and kissed him soundly on the cheek, then turned back to her locker. "I really do have to get going." She shut it closed, then smiled at him again. He winked back at her.

She was gathering her clothes and then her purse. She could feel his eyes on her. *What was on earth is on this fool's mind?* she wondered. She soon found out.

"I do need to ask you something, sister. Why did I just see you coming out of my office? What were you looking for?"

Jacob was feeling a bit more confident today. When he'd last seen Kimberla, he was upset. It may have been because he had confronted her vixen ass after not having much sleep. Or it may have been because he was feeling her so deeply. It had to be mental, or maybe it wasn't, but she made his heart beat so fast every time he was with her.

After he left he felt whipped. Everyone knows that the faster your heart beats, the more oxygen you use up. He went back home to get some much-needed sleep. Jacob was getting to that burned-out point. He tried sleeping but ended up twisting and turning restlessly on the couch. In the midst of his sad attempt to sleep he got a call from Michael asking him to meet later that evening at Mackings. Michael had been doing that a lot lately, asking for impromptu meetings and going over details about their soon-to-be large delivery of product.

The great thing about it was the closer time got to the big shipment, the more meetings they had about it. And the more meetings they had about it, the closer Jacob would be to putting an end to all this. He would nail Michael Riley and put the fucker away in a jail cell, where he belonged. But most importantly, at least to the DEA and FBI, Jacob would finally be able to nail Senator David Huggins.

He decided to keep most of the information he had found out about Huggins on the DL. Basically he didn't want to go to headquarters about it until he had more concrete proof of the senator's involvement.

So much was riding on this. A year of undercover work was too hard and he meant to do more than nail one or two fancy-talking slime heads and get a popular politician in hot water. Jacob wanted to make it all count. He wanted to shut down the whole crime dynasty of money, murder, drugs, and prostitution that Michael Riley had built. And he wanted to make sure he had every name, every filthy politician who worked with Michael, to get what they had coming to them.

The evening sun had already started to go down. The whole spirit of New York City was so different from any place Jacob had ever lived. Once the city clock read 5:00 P.M. or later, a city that was already buzzing with people everywhere became even more hectic.

He parked his large SUV in the back lot of Mackings, got out, and with long-legged strides made his way quickly inside to talk to Michael.

Jones met him at the back-door entrance, looking rather sweaty.

"Wassup, man?" Jacob said, reaching his hand out to Jones in a tight grip.

"You here to see Mike?"

"Yeah."

Jones eyes got big. "Is he here already?" he asked, looking around himself oddly.

"Why are you so worried about Mike?"

Jacob walked past Jones, trying to make his way down the hall with Jones steadily behind him. He noticed that he had still not been answered.

"Oh, oh. Don't tell me you still wrestling with the ladies on the job?" Jacob laughed. "You trying to get your ass fired, man."

"Oh, come on, you know how it is."

Jones, even with his vocal bravado, was still looking around, fidgeting nervously.

"Well look," Jacob said, "I have to go find him. You"—he pointed to Jones's chest—"best stop using Mike's place of business as a hoe house or you may end up jobless. Security is tops with him, you know this."

Not really responding, Jones walked past Jacob, seemingly in a rush to get back to "Heaven."

Jacob laughed and headed for Mike's office. Once he was there and noticed it was empty he went to the back room to look for him.

"Now, Mike, I know you didn't get me to come all the way down here for nothing. Where the hell are you?" he called out. He heard voices as he passed the ladies' dressing room, backed up, then tapped softly on the door before walking inside. The first person he saw was Kimberla and then Michael Riley. What perplexed Jacob the most was that they were not standing alone, but in each other's arms. He felt his whole body contract and before he could catch himself, words exploded from his mouth.

"What the fuck is this?"

18

The wiper blades swung angrily back and forth. The night storm that poured down on the city made it hard for Kimberla to see as she sat quietly beside Jacob. Although her work had always been dangerous and somewhat stressful, this was the first time that the stress stemmed from personal issues rather than being work related. At least she got the feeling it was personal, seeing that Jacob wasn't speaking to her at all.

She sighed, hoping to grab his attention. *Well that didn't work,* she thought to herself as he continued to ignore her. He was trippin'. Why was he trippin'? It wasn't as if he had caught her and Michael doing anything. He knew that everything she did in association with Mackings or Michael was all part of her alias. Besides, he wasn't her man or anything. They were not together. Yes, they had been together sexually, and no, that was not part of the job, but the Negro had no papers on her. No man did. That was just the way she liked it. Men were back-scratchers pure and simple. And that's all Jacob had been to her, pure and simple.

Hmph, she thought. If he wanted to act childish and imma-ture and ridiculous that was his prerogative. Men got on her last nerve. Give a lil bootie and they lose their freakin' minds. And what do they give in return? Absolutely nothing! If he wanted to act mad, she didn't care.

God . . . she couldn't take it anymore.

"Jacob, are you going to act like this all the way to Brooklyn?"

"I'm concentrating on the road," he responded back in a clipped tone. "I can't look at you and make sure we don't run into a pole at the same time. Besides, it's not like you're over there talking away." He glanced over at her. "I guess you're super tired from the evening's activities with Mike, huh?"

"No, I'm not tired at all. I haven't been doing anything to get tired, Jacob."

"Yeah, okay."

Kimberla sighed again. "You know you messed up, don't you? Going off on Michael like that. God knows what he must be thinking right now. Why the hell did you take it so personally? We were just talking!"

Jacob pulled up to her apartment building and shut off the ignition.

"Tell me something. Since when has kissing Mike's ass been part of your self-imposed undercover work here, Kimberla?" He shook his head in confusion. "I thought that we were to make him think we are together. Not only so that we could spend time and stay close without drawing suspicions, but also to make Mike see it's a hands-off situation so that he would keep his hands off you?"

"I didn't do anything with him. Plus, he even mentioned himself about us being together. So that charade is working."

"Charade, huh?"

"Isn't that what we're doing?" Kimberla spoke slowly.

"I guess . . ."

Jacob's tone was off. He almost sounded hurt. Although he had told her he cared about her, Kimberla knew she had to be wrong in her assessment of him. She just knew he wasn't feeling hurt because she had let Michael hug her. That would mean he had deeper feelings for her. That could not be. Men never had any feelings for Kimberla Bacon other than fear, admiration, or, as in the case of Malcolm Johnson, jealousy.

"I don't like this, Kimmy. I don't like the feelings I felt when I saw him touching you . . ."

"And what feelings were those?"

Kimberla could feel her face getting hot and she didn't know why. The temperature was not that warm this night.

Jacob reached over and caressed her cheek tenderly.

"Is that really all we have been doing? Has it all only been a charade—a cover for you?"

"You know me." She laughed. "I'm on the job twenty-four-seven. It's who I am."

She carefully avoided his eyes. But her face burned where he had caressed her.

"Woman, you know what I'm talking about," Jacob said. His voice cracked with the sudden intensity of the moment.

His hand moved down farther; rubbing, stroking, and caressing the nape of her neck. Kimberla shivered.

"When this is all over what's gonna happen with us?" Jacob asked. "Job well done and it's over between us as well?"

"I don't know."

"You go your way and I go mine? And yes, Kimmy, you do know. You know what you are feeling. And I think you're just scared."

Kimberla looked at Jacob defiantly. "Oh yeah? Scared of what? I'm not scared of anything or anyone!"

"Scared of being a woman; scared of feeling something for someone else; scared of needing a man for anything besides sex; scared of feeling weak."

He had her pinned. Damn him! But he wasn't correct, Kimberla mumbled in her mind. He wasn't!

"Why, Kim?" Jacob continued. "Why do you have to wear a mask? You're not really a chameleon because you're too set in your ways." He paused, then looked at her knowingly. "But then again, maybe you are. Chameleons change their skins according to their environment to protect themselves. The question is what are you hiding from? What are you protecting and why?"

"I'm not. I'm not!"

"Yes, you are."

Kimberla took a deep breath and swallowed repeatedly. Hell no she wasn't gonna cry. Not in front of a man; not in front of Jacob. Her mind went backward to all the taunts and teasing she had taken from girlhood onward. All the mockery she had endured when she was younger because she wasn't girly enough. Because she was tall, because she was dark, and because she was smart. All the things that guys didn't like in a female, she was and had always been. Back then she froze her mind and never allowed it to weaken. The only time she had weakened, the only time, had been at Georgetown University when she'd looked into the eyes of a tall, dark, gorgeous man that she could not have. The man sitting beside her at this very moment.

No, nothing had happened to make her hate men or anyone. But her childhood and especially her college years had not endeared her to the romantic part of life either.

"Kimberla, what are you thinking about? You haven't answered my question."

Without warning Kimberla opened the passenger door, then jumped out of the SUV quickly. She had to get away. The whole conversation with Jacob was too much; her thoughts about the painful past and growing up ugly and insecure were too much. That time had passed. And the ugly duckling she had once been had evolved into a swan. But deep inside when she looked in the mirror, though she tried to convince herself that she was smart and beautiful, most times she still saw that ugly duckling.

She barely made it into her building and to her apartment before Jacob stopped her. Kimberla sighed as he wrapped his arms around her. The tingles began to resurface.

"Let me go."

"Let me inside your mind; your heart," Jacob whispered back.

Kimberla turned around to face him. His eyes read tender, and some other unspoken emotion. For some reason that hidden emotion made her begin to spill her heart.

"You want to know why I'm the way I am?" she demanded. "Society made me tough. And growing up made me even tougher. When you grow up being teased by the opposite sex and told that you are ugly and unfeminine, you make up for what you lack by strengthening what you do have." Kimberla looked up at Jacob pleadingly. "I've always had my brains, Jacob. My intelligence. So what am I supposed to do now, huh? Make a mockery of that intelligence by falling all over the place over some man? When you are the ones that made me feel like less than a person?"

"No." She shook her head vehemently. "I can't do it. If I was to become some begging female, desperate for a man and willing to get hurt in order to get down with him, I would be no different and I am totally my own person."

"I never made you feel less than a person, Kim . . ."

"No, you didn't. I was just invisible to you. You didn't see me at all." Kimberla closed her eyes and breathed out slowly. "I need to go. It's getting late and I want to take a ba—"

Her attempted last word was swallowed up by Jacob's lips. He didn't just kiss her, he devoured her. His tongue danced inside her mouth, stroking her to a feverish pitch.

Kimberla needed this. She needed this kiss; this man. She needed Jacob.

As the oh-so-sweet kiss ended and Jacob pulled away slightly, Kimberla turned and unlocked her apartment door. They were both quiet as they stood looking at each other.

"So, am I invited to come in?" Jacob finally asked.

She looked at him and smiled slightly. She wanted him; she needed his dark body over hers. But somehow she wasn't feeling as confident as she had always felt when it came to men and sex. She knew it was because she had revealed so much of herself to Jacob. When someone had knowledge of your inner thoughts and feelings, they had power over you. But when

Jacob walked inside behind her, then led her to her bedroom, she followed, not even caring about the power he now had over her. When he took off her clothes, layer by layer, she let him. And when he made beautiful, sweet love to her body and soul, she cried.

19

Brooklyn, New York

The following day it was still raining, but for the first time in years Jacob was smiling and feeling sunny inside. The night before with Kimberla had been incredible. He had every reason to know and believe she was feeling him just as deeply as he felt her.

The woman had heat like a volcano, yet when she was wearing her so-called shield of protection she was chilly as snow.

Jacob looked in the mirror as he dressed in dark green slacks and a matching light green shirt. He was looking distinguished today; his normal everyday gear was jeans, khakis, or the regular run-of-the-mill casualwear.

There were three days until the big shipment drop of Michael Riley and David Huggins. Three days before everything would come to a final head. The meeting with Mike, which he was getting dressed for, would hopefully open up the rest of the puzzle. Like how he managed to get Huggins involved in his drug scheme, and who else was involved. It would also hopefully answer other whodunit questions. Like what happened to Agent Margo Hunter and the other legitimate Mackings dancers who had also disappeared. The fact that David Huggins was involved with Michael Riley also made Jacob suspicious that he could have something to do with the other disappearances in the city.

He brushed at the waves in his hair; changed the small, gold hoop earring he had worn the day before to a small, diamond stud; then grabbed his keys and made way for the door.

The ride from his apartment in Crown Heights to Houston's, one of Michael's favorite Manhattan restaurants, was mind busy for Jacob. No matter how hard he tried not to believe it, he couldn't shake the realization of what he had discovered the night before. It hit him the moment he moaned out Kimberla's name as his orgasm hit. He was falling in love with her.

All the years since Regina and Bali's death he never imagined he could crack back open, even an inch, those feelings he thought he reserved only for his deceased wife. It shouldn't have been a surprise. Kimberla was the first woman since his wife whose strength and passion could even remotely measure up to his. He wanted an equal—not some prima donna who answered every request with a yes, my lord, no, my lord. But Kimberla Bacon was completely her own person.

The problem was that she was so afraid, so very afraid. She would never admit it but Jacob could see her clearly. He wanted her, needed her to be willing to open her heart up to him and not just her bed.

Jacob pulled up to the crowded parking lot and surprisingly spotted Michael's car. It was a rare for Mike to ever drive himself anywhere. Michael Riley loved to look like the big man around town, limo and all.

"Good afternoon," the host said as Jacob walked up to the registration desk. "Welcome to Houston's. Will you be dining alone?"

"No, actually I'm here to meet someone. Is there a Michael Riley already here? He's expecting me."

"Ahh, yes." The host looked down at his register tablet. "You must be Mr. Simmons." The man looked back up at

Jacob, who was nodding in the affirmative, and smiled. "Right this way, sir."

They walked over to a corner display of tables that had a beautiful view of Manhattan. Michael smiled as he spotted Jacob.

"Hello, brother," he said, standing up and giving him a tight bear hug. "I was hoping you wouldn't stand me up."

"Why would I want to do something like that?" Jacob gave him a hug in return and then sat down. He watched, feeling his skin crawl, as Michael paused for a moment and took a big gulp of his Apple Martini.

"Last time we talked, Jonathon, you weren't too happy with me." Michael raised an eyebrow. "I have to admit I was shocked. Not only that you would talk to me in such a way, but then again your gutsiness is what makes me trust you. But also, I would never have thought a man of your intelligence would fall so hard for one of our naked, *dancing* ladies. No matter how appealing she may be."

"Would you like to order?" A short, blond waitress broke in, looking directly at Jacob.

"I'll have a gin and tonic, easy on the rocks, please. And bring me the hot wings; ranch dressing instead of blue cheese, and heavy with the celery." He looked at Michael. "Have you ordered yet?"

"Nope. You know I always wait for you."

He looked over at the waitress, who up to this point seemed to be ignoring him and focused entirely on Jacob. "Give me a large Caesar with seasoned shrimp. Oh, and I'll have another martini."

After the waitress left, Michael continued with his thoughts. "What's so special about Alisha?"

Jacob cringed. He had been worried that Michael would bring that up.

"It's not about her, Mike. Just I didn't know you were interested like that. Plus you knew I was chillin' with her."

"But I didn't know you were so serious about it."

The waitress popped up with their drinks and the conversation drew to a halt. Jacob was trying to think of what he could say to Mike. It seemed as if Kimberla was right: Jacob's overreaction had been a mistake and the cause of the uncomfortable questions about them. To say or pretend that he didn't care would make Michael feel that she was fair game. Kind of the way Lia was. Jacob had known for a long time that Mike was sexin' her, too. But he couldn't have him even imagining that he was gonna do the same with Kimberla.

"It's not that I'm so serious about her," Jacob finally said. "I just don't like to share my tuna. Shit, I'm already sharing Lia witcha ass." He laughed. Michael laughed back, seemingly convinced.

"It's cool. We're brothers, man. I won't poach in your frying pan if you aren't feeling it, okay? Never would we be fighting over no bitches. But that is a sexy piece you got there in Alisha." Michael winked.

Jacob ignored that comment.

"Now on to business. I told you way back we had a lot of shit about to go down and now is the time. Three more days, brother."

Jacob grimaced at the overabundance of gin in his drink, but started to feel excited at Mike's words.

"What made you decide to start trusting me, Mike?"

"I've always trusted you. But there is a time and place for everything. You know how I work." Michael stretched languidly. "Besides I had to be sure I could trust my partner. You, there was never a matter of trust involved."

Jacob had to fight hard not to smile at that comment.

"So by partner I take it you mean David Huggins?"

Michael nodded. They both waited quietly as their food was placed on the table. It seemed their waitress was moving incredibly slow which made Michael finally look at her in annoyance and say, "Are you done? We're in a private conversation here that we would like to get back to sometime today."

"Um . . . sorry." She gulped. Her cheeks reddened. She gave Jacob one final look of longing, then walked off quickly.

"You should hunt her down before we leave and get her to suck your dick in the bathroom. She looks desperate enough to pay you." Michael laughed.

Jacob chuckled back. "You crazy, man."

"But I'm right. You saw the hungry way she was looking at you." He leaned forward and pointed to Jacob's food. "She thought you were one of those wings there and wanted to suck ya bone."

"I don't care how she was looking at me. I have nothing against white folks but I'm not trying to do their women. I'm a seriously pro-black male. Especially when it comes to the women; I have no OJ inclinations. Now, like I said, I respect all women, but I *love* black women."

"And I'll toast you to that!" Michael brought his martini glass up for his toast. "But, a mouth and tongue have no color to me. They all give you the same results; getting that nut!" He winked again.

I'm getting sick of this nigga winking at me, Jacob thought. *Fag* . . .

"Okay, enough with that talk," Jacob said out loud. "You were talking about Huggins. Don't you feel you can trust him?"

"Fuck no! I don't trust politicians."

"So how did you two get involved? And why are you dealing with him if you don't trust him?"

Michael put a large amount of salad in his mouth, chewed it slowly, and then swallowed. He wiped his mouth with a napkin and said, "He came at me with an offer I couldn't refuse."

"And that was?"

"Jonathon, I've wanted to expand my operation for quite some time now. Everything we are doing here is funded mainly from our narcotics operation. Yours and Mario's gigs. You see why you two are so important to me?"

"I guess." Jacob coughed out a laugh.

"Anyhow, with customs cracking down as hard as they have been it's affected not only the amount of product we have to sell but also the quality. I won't be beat out by some young-ass, lil niggas who have balls enough to risk their freedom to get better product, regardless of the risk. The difference between me and the lil hoodrats is that I'm smarter. I'm smart enough to know how to handle my business."

"What offer did Huggins give you that you couldn't refuse?"

Michael continued on as if he hadn't even heard Jacob's question.

"I'm opening two new clubs and they are gonna be twice as big and twice as expensive to run." He shrugged his shoulders. "Basically, money is always an offer I can't refuse, but I don't let it consume me. That would make me what? Like them, right? Anyhow we are talking millions of dollars here."

"And Huggins's cut is half?"

Michael laughed at his question as if it were a joke. "Brother, please. I'm not about to share half of anything with that slimy bitch. His pay is fifteen percent."

Shaking his head incredulously Jacob said, "You mean to tell me that David Huggins—Senator David Huggins—has been willing to risk his life and his career for a measly fifteen percent?"

"Jonathon, you have to know that there is no politician who doesn't have ulterior motives. You also know that the senator is running for governor, or wants to."

"And?"

"And not all in his distinguished party are happy with him or were willing to endorse his nomination bid. What he has been getting out of this is his fifteen percent and also my people convincing his opponents to change their minds and endorse him."

Jacob's mind was spinning. It was all starting to make sense now. Michael Riley had been strong-arming Huggins's political rivals. It didn't take a genius to start adding up names of who had pull with the Senate to see who these rivals were. He would bet anything that Alan Mitchell was one of them.

"How have you been convincing them?" he finally asked Michael.

"What has a man's weakness always been, Jonathon?"

"Sex?"

"Bingo. And I have every type of woman any man could

ever want. I simply gave them what they wanted. But getting laid has been the downfall of men in power from Kennedy to Clinton. Nobody wants to be caught with his dick in his ear. So, all in all? I gave them an offer they couldn't refuse."

Michael smirked, and drained his martini glass.

20

Brooklyn, New York

Kimberla was dressed and ready for her evening performance. She had talked to Malcolm Johnson earlier and the conversation hadn't left her in the best of moods. She didn't want that to show in her dance though, even though she knew things were winding down. It bothered her that with all the work she had done to find out what happened to Margo, she was being blocked out. At least that was the impression she got from her conversation with Malcolm, and also with Jacob.

"Tell me about this Delphi person," Malcolm had said earlier in the day.

"I already told you she can be trusted. Delphi is a beautiful person."

Malcolm smirked. "I just bet she is; as beautiful as any hooker could be."

"Well, that hooker is the one who told me what happened to Margo. That gives her big cool points in my book!"

Malcolm had scoffed at that. His face always turned red in the cheeks no matter what emotion he felt.

"We already knew what had happened to Agent Hunter,

Kimberla. We didn't need you and some hoochie dancer finding out for us."

Lawd, the man irked her, Kimberla thought, coming back to the present. She fumed to herself, then laughed, thinking about how she had kindly showed his red ass to the door of her apartment. That had been two hours earlier. Now was a different place and time. Now Kimberla was more concerned about performing and getting it over with so she could get home and listen to Michael Riley's conversation of the night.

That's what had her feeling so high and so hyped. She also felt like she needed to talk to Jacob. She was realizing that even with all the work and effort she'd put forth, it wasn't doing any good because Jacob was holding back so much from her. Kimberla understood that he was nervous about possibly blowing his cover, but still. When he first discovered she was in New York, she was under the impression, from what he said, that they would rub each other's backs, so to speak. It was all becoming too much a secret musical-chairs game for her.

Kimberla jumped. She was in the bathroom stall, fighting with the back ties of her miniskirt when she heard her cell phone playing its R. Kelly tone. *Damn!* she thought, *I forgot to set it on vibrate.* She rushed out of the stall to pick it up. She didn't want anyone to see her cell ringing and perhaps look at the face of it and take notice of anyone who may be calling her.

She grabbed her phone, not realizing that the mini she was wearing was still untied. It fell to her ankles, tripping her slightly. She looked up and there was Lia. *Shit, did the girl have to always be up in her grill?*

"Thought I had tied that," she said with a laugh.

Lia looked from her to her phone, rolled her hazel eyes, and walked out the door with a slam.

"I can't stand you either," Kimberla said out loud although she was basically talking to herself.

She picked up her still-ringing cell phone, which had an unavailable flashing on the front plate. All her racing to get it was for nothing.

"Hello?"

"Are you by yourself?" Malcolm Johnson whispered over the line.

Kimberla looked around just to make sure. "I am now," she responded. "What's up?"

"I wanted to feed you a little something. We've found out from underground sources that Agent Hunter was executed in conjunction with a Senator Alan Mitchell. Same time, same place. And Riley was the smoking gun behind it all."

"What did she have to do with Alan Mitchell?" Kimberla asked.

"Well, the basis of Margo's assignment was to investigate a string of disappearing Mackings dancers. She was last contacted by Alan Mitchell. His charred remains washed up on the banks of the harbor today. It's all being kept on the hush for now, and till we get you out of New York, we don't want to scare Riley away." Malcolm paused and made a sucking noise. His greedy ass was always eating, Kimberla thought. "And even though my being rid of you would save me a lot of sleepless night and pains in my ass, Kyte doesn't want anything to happen to you like what happened to Margo either."

"Nothing is gonna happen to me, Malcolm. No one here knows who I really am so you can end your precelebration. Kimberla Bacon is gonna haunt your ass for life." She smiled slightly, although she was feeling quite ill inside.

Delphi had told her before that it was suspected that Margo's body was burned. With the discovery of Alan Mitchell's charred remains, the suspicion of the horror of her friend's death was more than just that, it was a guarantee. She only hoped that Margo was not tortured, and was dead long before they lit the match.

"Listen, I need to get going. I have to dance. But I will call you when I get home."

"Kyte wants you back in D.C., Kimberla," Malcolm insisted.

Maybe they were right, Kimberla thought. Coming to New York had mainly been for her own peace of mind. It was next to impossible to make the bust she wanted to make with so many legal odds stacked against her. The only way she had possibly helped the Bureau was by getting Delphi to open up. Now she would be a witness once they had Michael. She suspected that it was more Malcolm who wanted her out of town than Kyte. Kyte would have called her on things himself.

"I'll let Michael know I'm needed at home and that I have to leave Mackings," she finally told Malcolm. "But I hope you know I'm not fooled by your jealous tirades. I know it's you. Be sure, Malcolm, once I'm back on the job, you still won't be special agent in charge. You may have the upper hand here but I've only been helping, and doing a good-ass job with it, too," she angrily snapped.

"If you say so." He laughed, then hung up the phone.

"Excuse me," Lia purred as she pushed her way past Heaven and her dancing partner, Starr.

She ignored their hostile stares. They were just some jealous bitches anyhow, like most of the dancers at Mackings. After all, she had front-row access to Michael, and any of their asses he was tapping were just sloppy seconds.

Lia walked with a gleeful strut as she headed to his office. She couldn't believe her luck. Chameleon, the bitch, was about to be drowned. She got to Michael's office and didn't knock, simply pushed the door open and walked in.

"What the fuck? How many times have I told you to knock, Lia," Michael spat out.

She wasn't even moved by his shouted words. He had another dancer in his lap who was kissing him all over his neck.

"Leave, bitch," Lia demanded her. "I have something to tell you, Michael."

"What is your problem?" Michael asked her.

Lia, however, was still addressing the dancer. "Yes, he wants you to leave." She looked to Michael. "For real, sweetie, you will want to hear what I have to tell you."

Michael gave the girl an abrupt nod. "I'll call you back later," he told her. He looked at Lia as Debra passed by her and left his office. "This better be good."

"It is. I overheard a conversation. We have an FBI snitch at Mackings."

"What you talking 'bout, sister?" Michael laughed as if she had said something extremely funny.

"Alisha is not who she says she is. Her name is Kimberla and she's some kind of agent. I heard her just now on the phone." Lia gave Michael a smug smile at his look of surprise.

"You're bullshitting me, right?"

"No, she's been bullshitting you."

The room held silence. Lia put her hands on her hips, waiting for Michael to respond. He didn't.

"Well, what are you gonna do about her?" she demanded.

"Have you told anyone else about this?"

"Only you, boo." She leaned forward into Michael's ear. "You should get Jon-Jon and Mario to kill her. I'd watch gladly."

Michael could feel himself simmering inside. He wondered why these FBI hoes thought they could just run up on his business and try to ruin him. The same shit had happened with the white bitch. He had had her taken care of, and if what Lia was saying about Alisha, or Kimberla, or whatever the fuck her name was, was true . . .

"Get outta here, Lia. I have to make a few calls."

"But what about what I just told you?" she asked indignantly. "You know you have to clue me in on what you're gonna do."

"The only thing I need you to do is be here early morning, around nine-thirty A.M. I want you to tell Jonathon exactly what you told me. I want the whole story. I have to wonder if he's on the up and up now, as close as he seems to be to Alisha."

"No, Michael, you know Jon is clean. He's been working with you a long time. It's her; she's the one."

Lia didn't want Michael turning on her baby Jon over the fact he had been fucking around with the agent. She had questions of her own, but she would protect Jonathon with her very life if need be.

"I believe he will be able to speak for himself, Lia. As things rest now, I just want to know what the fuck is going on. Go on out there. You are dancing after Alisha. Act as normal as possible."

Lia turned to walk away.

"Lia."

"Yes?" She turned back to look at Michael.

"Don't allow your jealousy to fuck you up. You understand?"

21

Brooklyn, New York

"Why have you been so absent from the club lately?"

Jacob swallowed a moan as Kimberla's soft hands massaged gently down the base of his spine.

"Do we really have to talk shop right now?" he asked softly.

Kimberla's lips followed where her hands had been, causing Jacob's mouth to open up, but no sound came out. His heart throbbed rapidly when he felt her warm lips and tongue bathing his backside. When she began to delve too deeply, followed by her fingers, he stopped her.

"What?" She laughed.

"That's some freaky shit you trying to do. Real men don't get their arses poked." Jacob looked uncomfortable, which only seemed to add to her delirious, tear-jerking laughter. "Is it that funny?" Jacob frowned.

"Yes! You're cracking me up. Real men? You know you like it. Turn around," she whispered. "Let me see what real men do like . . ."

Jacob laughed, but turned around so she could have her playground. It was early morning when he had knocked on her door. The evening before was spent in conference at a hidden DEA meeting, splitting heads with his superiors about some of the new events that were unfolding. After he left he couldn't wait to see Kimberla. She was an addiction to him and as soon as she'd opened the door he let her feel how hooked he really was.

Her soft lips were all over him. His chest, stomach, licking slowly to his groin. He moaned deeply when she went down to his manhood, licking him softly yet firmly.

"Like that, baby," he gasped out. "Just like that."

The little moans and purrs that came from Kimberla turned him on almost as much as the magic she was creating with her mouth. He threw his head back against the pillows, then laced his finger through her hair, arching his body upward as she sucked him harder, deeper.

"Oh shit!" Jacob cried. Kimberla took him deeper still and his body jerked. "Oh shit!" he moaned again. The tingling throb started to build in his testicles and he was almost there.

Suddenly Kimberla stopped, moved on top of him, and slid down his hard manhood. Her velvet folds enveloped him in a tight blanket of heat. Up and down she rode him, causing him to have to grab hold of her slim hips as if he were gripping a horse's reins. She balanced herself on the balls of her feet and took him in deep. He could hear her throaty moans as she rocked and rolled, grinded and gripped him. Sweat dripped down between her nipple-erect breasts.

Of all the women Jacob had been with, and there had been many, he had never known one as raw and hungry as Kimberla. Even though they were doing this together, it was as if she was using his body for her pleasure. She made no apologies for it, and it turned him on. He was being thoroughly fucked.

"Take what you want, baby," he mumbled between clenched teeth. "Just take it."

He could tell she was about to come from the way her body started shaking uncontrollably. And he knew for a fact she was there when he felt her inner walls grabbing and releasing, squeezing him like a vice, inside her. That set off his orgasmic explosion.

"Ahh, Kim! Yeah, baby! Oh . . ." He jerked again and again.

Both of them lay there, fighting to catch their breath. As she got hers Kimberla kissed Jacob's neck tenderly and looked into his eyes. He felt she wanted to say something but couldn't.

"What is it?" he whispered, wiping the hair from her forehead that was matted with sweat.

"Nothing, it's just." She paused. "Nothing . . ."

"It's good between us, isn't it?" Jacob waited a second before he added, "Kim, I want to see you after this is all over. I want to get to know the real you—the real Kimberla Bacon. Do you want that, too?"

"Then what?" she asked. She was looking at him with slight fear in her eyes.

"Then maybe you will see, as I do, that this is more than just sex. There is a lot more going on with us."

"I do see that. But what is it that you want, though? What do you see happening?"

Jacob's cell phone rang before he could answer her question. That seemed to give Kimberla some relief.

"Hold up," he said. Kimberla lay back against the covers, pulling the cool sheet over her naked body.

"Hello?"

"Jonathon, I've been trying to contact you since last night." It was Michael Riley.

"Wassup, Mike?"

"I need you to come to my office right away."

Jacob looked over at the alarm clock beside Kimberla's bed.

"Right now? It's eight-thirty in the morning."

"Obviously not too early for you to be getting your groove at Alisha's place, or whatever her name is," Michael said sarcastically.

Or whatever her name is?

Mike's words made Jacob sit up quickly. What would make him say that the way he said it?

"I'm on my way. Give me thirty minutes, okay?"

"You need to get here, brother. Come on out of the pussy. I'll see you in *twenty* minutes."

Michael hung up the phone, not giving him time to reply. Jacob reached across Kimberla, putting his cell down.

"I gotta go," he said to her.

"Why? I thought we were going to breakfast? Not to mention we were in a deep conversation just now."

Her expression was one of confusion. Yet her response confused Jacob also. From the standoffish reception he got from her whenever he tried to talk about a possible deeper relationship between them, one would think she'd be glad to have the convo interrupted. Would he ever really understand women?

"How 'bout I call you after lunch?"

"Was that Michael on the phone?" Kimberla pressed.

"Yeah, it was." He made his way to the bathroom as he said this, going for a quick washup. Kimberla followed carefully behind him.

"So what did he want?"

Jacob didn't answer. His mind was all over the place. Michael was suspicious of Kimberla. That meant that Jacob's association with her placed him under suspicion, too. A year. A whole year of undercover work and now just days before he caught his prey, things were starting to fall apart. Hell no! He had worked too damn hard and too damn long!

"What did he want, Jacob?"

Jacob looked at her and started slipping his jeans on. "Why you trippin'?"

"I'm not tripping. Just your whole tone and demeanor has changed since that phone call. One minute you are warm and loving, saying how you want us to see each other after this is all over, and the next minute you're making waves to get out of here."

Jacob brushed past her, rushing to get his shoes on. Minutes had passed since he talked to Mike. He had to get to Mackings. He didn't dare tell Kimberla what was going on. What would she do? Try to get all up in things, he knew. That's how they got in this situation in the first place. It was her persistence in knowing everything and in doing everything herself.

"I have to go," he finally said. He kissed her softly on the cheek. "I'll call you later."

"But, Jacob," she shouted from the door, "wait!"

"I'll call you," he mouthed, and disappeared.

There was so much tension in the room. Jacob felt it. He sat quietly and listened while Lia described to Mike and him the phone conversation she had overheard between Kimberla and some other person. He wondered who the person could be, but suspected it was Malcolm Johnson. The feds were fucking him up!

"She jumped when her cell rang. Running out the stall like some lunatic." Lia laughed nastily. "I guess she didn't expect to see me."

"And what was said?" Michael asked.

"Oh, she was going on about how she almost has all the information she needs. And how she's gonna nail you." Lia looked at Michael. "Then she was kind of arguing with the person on the phone. She was going on about how when she is done here and is back in D.C., she'll still be special agent in charge. So I guess she's some type of big wheel with the FBI."

"You got all that from just listening to a phone conversation?" Jacob asked.

"I hope you aren't defending her, brother."

Jacob looked at Michael who had just spoken. "It's not that I'm defending Alisha—"

"Which is not even her real name, by the way," Lia cut in.

Jacob seriously wanted to slap her ass. But at the moment he wasn't sure who he wanted to slap the most, her or Kimberla, for being so careless. He had to play it all off. The look in Michael's eyes let Jacob know he had to make it good.

"Did you have any idea or suspicion about her, Jonathon?" Mike asked.

"No, I didn't. This has me just as surprised as it does you, man."

"Okay. Listen, Lia, I appreciate you clueing me in on things. Good looking out. But you can leave now."

Lia's eyes grew big. She stood up, placing her hands on her hips. "What about Chameleon? What are you gonna do about that bitch? You're gonna kill her, right?"

"I'm done talking to you about this, Lia," Michael said slowly, but purposely. "Go home."

Lia stomped across the room mumbling obscenities. She looked back at Jacob and Michael, walked out the door, and slammed it.

Once they were alone Michael got up and walked over to his wet bar.

"Drink?" He motioned to Jacob.

"No, I'm good. Too early for me."

"Fine. Let's talk."

22

Brooklyn, New York

Michael's office was always chilly. He liked it that way. He said it always reminded him that he was alive, whereas heat always reminded him that he would surely go to hell when he died. The coolness had Jacob shaking a bit now. He started to ask Mike to turn the air conditioner down some but didn't want to request too much. He wasn't sure of his standing at this point. Either way you threw it he needed to make Mike believe he was not necessarily devastated, but surprised about Kimberla.

"I'm feeling really bad."

Jacob swallowed the lump that had started to form in his throat. It wasn't that he was scared of Michael. There were just the two of them in the building. If it came down to a fight between them Jacob wouldn't even need a weapon, which he kept on his person at all times. He could strangle the life out of Mike's lungs with his bare hands.

"What you feeling bad about?" Jacob asked. "Alisha? I am, too. I can't believe this shit. I mean I was just with her."

"No, I feel bad because you are like a brother to me and I don't know what to think and believe right now."

"So what is this? You don't trust me, Mike? Because I was

fooled by a beautiful woman that you brought into the family?" Jacob formed a hurt expression on his face and said in a shocked, hurt voice, "Yeah, you should feel bad. I've given you nothing but loyalty, man!"

Michael moved slowly around his marble desk, sipping his drink. He was a man of impeccable taste and it showed in all he did and in everything he owned.

"I'm concerned because you were sleeping with her. She had to have bled you a little for information. I need you to tell me everything you know."

Everything he knew. Jacob's mind rolled quickly to assess what he should say. He knew that in order to take suspicion off of him and keep his cover he would have to appear to be against Kimberla. Doing that would also mean keeping it all from her. Michael would for sure be keeping an eye on Kimberla and working out a way to get rid of her. Jacob knew he had to convince her to leave New York immediately.

"I don't have anything to tell you, man," Jacob finally said.

Michael looked at him as if trying to find the secrets in his mind. A whole year of trusting someone with all your secrets was hard to shake when it came down to it. But Jacob knew Mike was no fool.

"What do you want to do about Alisha? She has to be taken care of."

"Do you want me to talk to her?"

"Talk to her about what?" Mike asked. "What I want you to do is find out for sure if what Lia is saying is true. And if it is I want you to *exterminate* her. And I want to *see* you do it."

"Why do you want me to do it?" Jacob choked out. *This is worse than I figured,* he thought to himself.

"I guess you can tell I'm not feeling too good about any of this, brother. If there are feds sliding into our lil family I have to know for sure who is on my side and who is not. If you are as loyal to me as you say you are, that loyalty will supersede anything you felt for Alisha. If she has been deceiving me, she's been deceiving you, too. You shouldn't even hesitate."

"You're right." Jacob ran his hands over his face as if tired.

"So work it out. Find out all you can about her, set it up, and get rid of her. Let me know the plans."

Jacob stood to leave. "I'll let you know something." He headed toward the door.

"Jonathon."

"Yeah," he said, turning back to Michael.

"Don't disappoint me."

The subway car was filled with passengers. Kimberla found herself standing and holding on tightly to the pole, waiting to get to the stop for Delphi's apartment. Her mind was busy wondering why Jacob had not called her.

This was the reason she kept her feelings to herself. Even though she hadn't vocalized her thoughts to Jacob he had to know how she felt. She had given it all to him that morning. Something wasn't right. The way he had jumped up and left without explanation. Had the emotions scared him? Did he see too much, feel too much from the way she had clung to him? She had tried calling his cell phone over and over before she finally decided to go see Delphi. And all she got was his voice mail.

Another thing that got to her is that she seemed to not have connected the bug on Michael's phone correctly. She wasn't doing anything right on this job, it appeared. How to get back into his office and reconnect it seemed almost an impossibility. She wasn't dancing tonight.

She did a quick prayer to Margo. *Things are coming together, sis. I don't know what the hell I'm doing, but it's all coming together and I won't let you down.*

The train rumbled and shook, causing Kimberla to grab hold of the arm of the man in front of her. He looked back and gave her a wicked smile. "Sorry," she mumbled, thinking how there was a freak behind every door in New York City.

Once the train stopped at her spot, Kimberla happily got off, holding her bag crossways over her chest. She wasn't too worried about getting mugged. Since she had been in New York she carried an "I dare you" look on her face. She dared anyone to try to touch her or anything on her person, or she would kick some serious bootie.

Kimberla got to Delphi's flat and knocked softly on the door. It opened with two taps.

"Hey there," Delphi said with a smile. "Come on in."

"Damn, you got it hot in here!"

Kimberla could feel sweat balls popping up at her hairline. It had been so hot walking from the train that she was looking forward to the cool air at Delphi's apartment. Seemed that wasn't to be. She went in and took a seat on the couch.

"I'm sorry. They cut my power off today." There was stress written all over Delphi's pretty face.

"What? Why? How much is your bill?"

"Two hundred and sixty-two dollars." Delphi sighed. "It's been hard, Kimberla. I didn't have that much saved and since there is no cash coming in, I've been totally at the mercy of no God."

Kimberla looked at her with a sad frown. She felt bad that Delphi helped her and the FBI with information about Mackings and Margo, yet was in the sad financial position she was in.

"I'm so sorry, girl. Why didn't you tell me things were so bad for you? I would have made sure you had the money for your lights and rent and whatnot."

"I'm not asking for handouts," Delphi replied. She was carefully avoiding Kimberla's eyes.

Kimberla placed her hand over hers and squeezed softly.

"It's not about taking a handout, it's about surviving. Truth of the matter is if I had not gotten you involved with helping me get dirt on Michael you probably would have found another job by now."

Delphi shook her head then ran her hands over her eyes and started massaging her temples.

"I'll get it straight," she said in a tired whisper. "But I wanted to talk to you about other things, not my light bill." She laughed.

Kimberla knew Delphi was trying to change the subject. She was pretty good when it came to reading real laughs compared to fake ones, and Delphi, beneath the laughter, was holding back tears.

"Okay," Kimberla relented, "I'll drop it for now. But we will get your electric bill paid and back on before the night is out!"

Delphi ignored that but grabbed Kimberla's attention when she told her, "I found out something juicy this morning. You know I'm not the only dancer Michael screwed over. There is this girl named Debra, she used to dance and work at The Dorm."

"Michael's little escort palace?"

"Yes." Delphi took out a Virginia Slim and lit it. "This is another habit I need to give up. I sure can't afford to smoke with cigarettes being seven-fifty a pack here."

"Come on, Delphi. We can talk about your cigarettes later. You know you have to finish telling me this."

"So, um . . ." Delphi blew smoke out through her nostrils. "Debra worked with Carly, your Margo. And she worked with another girl named Benita. We all called her Beebe. See Michael had Beebe and some other girls on this specific job. Fucking around with these senators and this judge, sleeping with them, blackmailing them."

"Wait," Kimberla said, putting her hand up in pause. "Blackmailing them for what? And where are Beebe and Debra now?"

"Debra is in hiding. Beebe, she's dead . . ."

"Why is she in hiding? And why is Beebe dead? What was this blackmailing scheme about, Delphi?" Kimberla pressed.

Delphi's hands were shaking as she put her cigarette out.

"Michael has a lot of political connections. He has one in particular—"

"David Huggins?"

"How did you know about him?" Delphi queried.

"Well I've been doing my homework and my own little investigating, too."

"Hmm . . . well Michael is in cahoots with him. They were using the girls at The Dorm; getting them to sleep with, videotape and then blackmail some of David Huggins's political rivals. Debra told me all this herself. The thing is, after Michael used the girls? They started disappearing, one after another. Some, like Beebe, just turned up dead."

Kimberla sat back on the couch and fought to catch her breath. This was Margo's case—the whole sordid deal. If Kimberla had only known from the start then it would have made things so much easier for her. Sometimes she felt unsure about the code of silence given undercover cases.

"Delphi, do you know the names of any of the politicians involved with this blackmail scheme?"

"Alan Mitchell was Beebe's John Boy." Delphi was rubbing her eyes again.

"And he was found dead . . ."

"Yeah."

Kimberla was busy thinking hard. "Anyone else?"

"No, but Debra did tell me that she was asked to hook up with someone. She refused and then she was threatened. That's why she ran into hiding. I don't know whatever happened with him."

"Who was he?"

"Ralph Carson. See they wanted Debra to get to him at first, but Senator Carson is not into women like that. He likes young men. Debra said they got this other lil white dude to do his thing with the senator."

"And where is this lil white dude?" Kimberla was almost afraid to ask.

Delphi looked up at her. "Why, he's dead. His name was Ronnie Jones."

Thirty minutes later Kimberla was rushing down the hot sidewalk trying to get to the station before she missed her train. She had been struggling to get Jacob on his cell from the moment Delphi mentioned Ralph Carson and kept getting nothing but his voice mail.

"Come on, Jacob!" she whispered to herself as his cell continued to ring.

"Hello?"

"Oh my God! I thought I would never get you. Where on earth have you been, man?" she cried.

Jacob was quiet for a moment.

"Jacob?"

"Where are you?" he asked.

"I'm on . . ." she looked up at the street sign, ". . . Twenty-third and Broadway. Where are you, Jacob?"

"That doesn't matter. Listen to me," he whispered. "I need you to meet me tomorrow at this warehouse in Crown Heights. It's on—"

There was a buzzing noise on either his cell or hers. Kimberla started panicking.

"Jacob? Jacob, are you there?"

The call was lost.

23

Brooklyn, New York

It was a good thing they had lost the connection. Jacob hated what he had to do. It was all for the sake of the case. Hopefully Kimberla would understand once it was all over. But for now he knew he would have to stress her out for a bit.

He pulled up to his Bronx apartment and let out a big sigh. Even though Mike was still calling him brother, Jacob knew there was a lot of second-guessing there. Mike wanting him to be the trigger on Kimberla was a big test. Jacob wished he could trust her enough to let her in on what was happening, but he couldn't. She was too involved emotionally; she was too hyper and she wasn't acting anything like the Kimberla Bacon he had always known.

After walking into his apartment Jacob went into the kitchen to make himself a snack. This had been the longest day of his life. In the morning he woke up in Kimberla's arms, making sweet love to her, or as some would call, fucking their brains silly.

He rethought the snack thing. Thoughts of their morning rump made him hard. Why oh why did she have to get caught talking on that damn cell phone? He almost had her, he knew it! Jacob could tell she had feelings for him but was holding them back. Now he had to fake plan her murder. Would she ever forgive him for holding back on her? He was also holding back on his superiors. He knew that if he told them everything that was going on they would pull him off the case, and basically everything would be down the drain.

After stripping his long, dark body of his clothes, Jacob went to take a hot shower. His phone rang.

Damn, he thought, grabbing the receiver.

"Hello?"

"Have you talked to the snitch?" It was Michael Riley.

Hell, I'm too tired for more of this shit, Jacob thought to himself.

"She called me before I got home. I told her to meet me tomorrow but we were cut off."

"So what is she up to now?" Michael asked.

"I don't know."

"Jonathon, you are supposed to know. I want you to keep an eye on her!"

"Shit, nigga, I am. Can I take a goddamn shower?" Jacob said heatedly. "She's gonna meet me tomorrow. I have to call her again because we lost the connection but I will have her at the warehouse tomorrow, okay?"

"Call her now."

"Now?"

"Yes, now."

"Who is it exactly that you don't trust, Mike, me or Alisha?"

Michael was sucking his teeth. That irritated Jacob.

"Do you know how much money is involved here, brother? Do you? Her name is Kimberla Bacon. She's a special agent. I got all the information on her. I want her ass dead."

"How do you know all this for sure?" Jacob asked.

"You know I have my connections. Once I had a first name, that's all it took. There is no doubt in my mind she was planted. It's not the first time this has happened. I really shouldn't be surprised. But I don't want any mishaps to occur here. Call her back, now."

"Okay, I will."

"Oh, and Jonathon?"

Jacob waited to see what Michael had to say, but his mind was already rolling.

"Yeah?"

"Tomorrow, I want to talk to her before you kill her. I want to find out if she has any helpers in the house. I don't care what you have to do to get it out of her."

Where there is knowledge, there has to be a plan. And Kimberla was the master at good planning. She stood up, looking at her extravagant clothes in the mirror. At times like this, her tall, uncurved body was her saving grace. She needed to make herself look like a man, trying to look like a woman. *How does a woman fake like she's a transsexual?* Kimberla asked herself. She was about to test herself to the limit.

She put on a big wig that was way over the top, but fit the bill perfectly. She put a tight wrap around her breast but loosened it some, as to appear to be growing, but not just there yet. And lastly, she put on the strap. Kimberla laughed to herself. She wasn't sure when she bought it if she wanted to be well endowed or just a lil bit there, then seeing she was to be a black transsexual, figured she would have a lil sumpin-sumpin for in case the senator tried to cop a feel.

After heavily applying makeup and testing her voice to make it on the deep side, she was ready. She picked up her sequence bag and walked out her front door, working her hips the way she had seen he-shes do in her outrageous line of undercover work.

It took a bit longer than it normally did for her to hail a cab, but after about fifteen minutes one had mercy on her and stopped. The cabby gave her an odd look, then a smile. That told her that her costume was doing the job. She let him know where she wanted to go.

"No problem," he said. "So, how long have you been a woman?"

"What makes you think I'm not a woman?" Kimberla said in a deep voice. She was cracking up inside.

"My bad." He smiled.

The dude was kinda cute. It's a shame she had to play him the way she was doing.

"So, you tricking or what?"

Kimberla's eyes got big. "What the hell is this?" she screamed indignantly. She looked around the cab. "Is this taxi-cab confessions or something? You want a hand job or something? Muthafucka, you wouldn't even be able to afford somebody of my class!"

"Okay, Miss, or Mister, or whatever you are. Again, my bad!"

"Hmph!"

She rolled her eyes in a gay fashion and ignored the cab driver. He seemed to get the hint. Then her cell phone rang.

"Yes?" she said, still speaking in her deeper voice.

"Kimberla?" It was Jacob.

"Hi, baby."

"Why you talking like that?"

"Just doing my thing, boo. What you need?"

Kimberla could see the cabby looking at her through the rearview mirror. It was a shame she couldn't tell Jacob what she was doing. But she knew he wouldn't approve.

"We got cut off earlier. I need to talk to you tomorrow. Things are coming to a head. I can't explain right now, but I need you to meet me at three," he said.

"Where do you want me to meet you?"

Jacob paused for a moment as if distracted by something. "Let's meet at Mackings. I'll explain when I see you. And oh, I don't know what you doing or wassup with the deep talking but off the record, hmm . . . Naw, I won't say it." He hung up.

"You turn me on, too, baby," Kimberla said, pretending she wasn't talking to a dial tone. "Buh-bye." She closed her flip phone and smiled wickedly at the cab driver.

Once she got to Ralph Carson's office she walked quickly past his secretary's desk, straight to his office door.

"Excuse me," the heavyset secretary said, "do you have an appointment?" She looked Kimberla up and down in disgust.

"No, I don't, and I don't need one." Kimberla crossed her fingers, hoped her pushiness paid off, and she didn't get thrown out on her ass. She kept on walking and pushed his door open. Ralph Carson was on the phone. He looked up at her in shock.

"Who the hell are you?" he shouted.

"You may not know who I am but I know who you are. And you knew my baby Ronnie, too," Kimberla rambled, moving her hands all over the place in a RuPaul style.

"Senator, I'm so sorry," his secretary said, rushing in front of Kimberla. "I'll get security right away!"

"You better tell your busybody to step back," Kimberla warned. "You'd better tell her. I got too much shit on you, Ralph Carson. You know you best to talk to me or I'm gonna do my talking to the papers."

"Abigail, hold up. Close the door." Senator Carson's feathers looked quite ruffled. "I want to see what this *person* has to say. Hold my calls, please."

Kimberla smiled inwardly. She strutted her hips over to the big leather chair sitting in front of his desk, sat down, and crossed her long legs.

After the door closed the room got quiet. Ralph Carson took a deep breath, and his eyes never left Kimberla. He reached into his cigar case and pulled out an import, then offered her one.

"No thanks, that's bad for your breath," she replied, making a face.

"But of course." He put the cigar back in the ivory case. His words came out in one quick sentence. "Who sent you here? What do you want and how much will it cost to get rid of you? I won't keep being blackmailed. You understand?"

"I don't know nothing about that shit. All I want to know is about my baby, who you were fucking. I want to know why he is dead, and I want to know who killed him."

"Who is Ronnie?" the senator asked, avoiding her eyes.

"Bitch, don't play games with me." Kimberla looked at him and sneered. "I know your type. The money you use to give my baby was paying for my hormone shots."

Ralph Carson's eyes bugged out at that comment. Kimberla laughed. "Uh-huh." She stood up and turned around in a slow circle. "I look good, too, don't I? Now my baby is dead and I want answers."

"Listen, lower your voice a little. I have a career to protect. This has all gone far enough. I have nothing to do with Ronnie Jones's murder," Ralph said in a trembling voice.

"But you have an idea who was blackmailing you, as you call it. Who was it? I want to know who hurt my boo. He was a good person!" She looked at him as if he was yesterday's garbage. "You undercover queens make me sick. Hiding and creeping on your wives, then chasing people like my Ronnie, trying to get poked. He was a good person!"

"That's not the way it was. We had a special relationship," Ralph Carson said softly. "I liked him. And I had nothing against him. But he did trick me. You have to understand I was a victim, just as he was."

Kimberla leaned over Ralph's desk in a threatening way. "Just give me a name. My peeps and I will take care of it. I may be a woman now or at least on my way, but trust me I can still kick ass like a man."

"I can't give you a name. I'm a senator. Can you imagine what will happen if any of this got out?"

"Can you imagine what will happen if you don't tell me what I want to know? Your name will get out anyhow. I'll have your gay ass on *The Morning Show*."

"I don't know. I don't know any names." The man was almost in tears. "All I can say is that I was forced to change my vote for the governor nomination, and that Ronnie was sent to me from this place called The Dorm. That's all I know, please!"

She wanted more, but the senator was crumbling. Kimberla looked at him and shook her head. It was a shame that men who claimed to be so strong and powerful, who swore they would do so much for their state and for the people, were nasty little perverts behind closed doors. As she always said, there was a freak behind every door in New York City; most of them resided in public office.

She got up from her seat, thanked the senator, and made her way out the door. Now she had to talk to Delphi's friend, Debra.

Ralph Carson was slowly feeling the weariness of his life. Everything he had worked for, all the years of struggle and now it had come down to this. Whoever this person was would surely put his business in the street. But it really didn't matter. If this transsexual knew about him and Ronnie Jones then the lowest of society knew. It wouldn't be long before everyone else did, too.

His mind slowly drifting away from him, Ralph Carson found himself standing on the edge of his office window, then he let go, and flew.

24

Brooklyn, New York

After her eventful night Kimberla collapsed in the bed, dreaming sweet dreams of Jacob. She was at the top of the Empire State Building. Dancing. Floating to the soft sounds of Kenny G's melody, "Songbird." She was dancing by herself but thinking of Jacob. She closed her eyes. When the song got to the middle chord she stopped and opened them. She turned to her right and there he was: six feet and five inches of tall, sweet chocolate milk. She saw his beautiful, dark face. She reached her hand out and he walked over to her, bowing at her feet as if she were a black queen.

"May I have this dance?" he asked softly.

Kimberla didn't respond. She simply took his hand in hers, dancing around and around in circles, letting the magic of the evening caress their souls.

When the song came to its end she was in his arms, looking in his eyes. His lips parted and he bent his head to hers and kissed her. Their tongues stroked and caressed each other, drawing life from each other. She felt her body melting into his. When he stopped kissing her she feared she was gone, her heart no longer belonging to Kimberla Bacon.

"I love, Jacob," she whispered. "I love you."

"I love you, too, Kimberla . . ."

Kimberla sat up in a rush. Her heart was beating so fast and the only thing that would come out of her mouth was, "What the hell?"

"Oh, lawd, I know that was a dream," she said out loud to herself.

Even though she had been dreaming it all, Kimberla wanted to cry. What did the dream mean? What did it mean when someone had become so vital a part of your life that you dreamt about them?

She stood up and put her powder-blue robe on, and then rushed to the bathroom to brush her teeth. She wanted to wash away not only morning breath, but the bad taste that dream had left in her mouth. She looked at her face. All the heavy makeup from the night before was gone, and she looked tired. She wondered deep down where that tiredness came from. Kimberla had done undercover work that was much more physically straining than this one. But then she knew the mental was heavier than the physical. What she wasn't sure about was whether it was the mental weight of losing her best friend that had her down or the mental weight of love.

She threw cool water over her face and then dried it softly with a towel. She reached for her face cream, hoping it would massage away some of her imagined stress lines, and jumped at the sudden banging at her door. The small jar fell into the sink.

"Who on earth could that be this time of the morning?' she said. She walked quickly to the door and looked out the peephole. It was Delphi.

"Girl, what is wrong?" she asked as she opened it. Delphi rushed inside.

"It's all over the news! Have you looked at the news yet?" Delphi cried.

"What is all over the news?"

Delphi didn't answer her. She rushed over to Kimberla's

small TV and clicked it on. It showed the outside of a government building, a nighttime broadcast. A body was covered with a white sheet and a familiar, heavyset secretary was standing with a news crew, crying.

"I don't know what happened." She sniffed. "I don't know why he would do this. There was this transsexual person there to see him but she left. That's all I know."

Kimberla's body grew cold.

"Can you describe her to us?" the news reporter asked.

"She was tall, that's all I know. Oh, God!" the woman cried.

Across the screen the scrawl read loud and clear. *Senator Ralph Carson found dead.*

They were to meet at David Huggins's east-side apartment to discuss the last-minute details of the cocaine drop. Mike had told Jacob that Huggins insisted that everything be organized perfectly.

Jacob was a bit irritated that he had rushed from home, getting up early, and Mike's car wasn't even in the parking lot. He pulled into the crowded lot and turned off his ignition. He wasn't sure if he should wait for Mike, or just go on by himself. After pondering the issue for a moment, he decided to go in and get to know a bit more about Huggins and how he got involved with a character such as Michael Riley.

He walked up and knocked at Huggins's condo door. It opened quickly.

"Where is Riley?" David Huggins asked, his face red.

"He's coming. But I'm here on time." Jacob walked in lazily. He reached his hand out to Huggins. "How've you been?"

"How have I been? How in the fuck do you think I've been? This is crazy!"

"What are you talking about?" Jacob was confused at his demeanor.

"You—you people are messing me up. What do you think is going to happen with Michael running around killing everybody? They are going to point the finger to me. Eventually they are going to think I've had something to do with all these murders and disappearances."

David Huggins looked like he was about to explode; his face turned an even deeper purple.

"That trigger-happy nigger. I should have known better than to get involved with the likes of him!"

"Whoa," Jacob said, drawing back a little in surprise. "Chill out with the N word. Here I thought you were a Democrat, a liberal?"

"This has nothing to do with politics!"

Huggins seemed to run out of energy. He sat back on his couch, breathing deeply. Jacob sat down beside him.

"Okay, why don't you tell me why you're so upset?" he asked him.

Huggins was quietly thinking things out. Finally he said, "It wasn't supposed to be like this, you know? I know I'm the right one for governor, and everyone else knows it, too. If Michael had simply stuck to our plans and if those damn haters had simply not been so greedy and stubborn, none of this would have happened." He put his hands over his face. "All my life. I've been waiting all my life for this chance. I'm ready! I just wanted things to be fair. I just wanted the people of New York to get a chance to see what I could do."

"Didn't you choose to work with Mike? He didn't force you to do anything you haven't wanted to do," Jacob noted.

David Huggins shook his head violently. "No one was supposed to get hurt. That was not the plan! Michael knew that."

"But you knew when you got involved with someone like him. You knew how he operated. And the money doesn't hurt either, does it?"

Jacob was having fun, pretending he knew all that Huggins was talking about. But the way he was spilling his guts, it wouldn't be long before Jacob did know all. *Oh, the tangled webs we weave,* he thought to himself.

"I don't trust him." David Huggins suddenly looked at Jacob warily. "I'm not sure I should trust you either."

"Then why are you telling me all this?"

"I don't know." He sighed. Suddenly he looked at Jacob. "Do you trust Riley?"

"I trust, me, Jonathon Simmons. If someone can benefit me we are cool."

"Then what if . . . what if I gave you an offer?" Huggins said timidly.

"What kind of offer?"

"After this is all over, I don't want your boss having anything over my head. I want it over and done with. I don't think that will be the case with him. I need him gone . . ."

He wanted Jacob to kill Michael. *This is some senator,* Jacob thought.

"You want him dead?"

"How much will it cost me?" asked Huggins slowly.

The doorbell rang.

"We can talk about this again later, okay?" Huggins said as he got up to answer.

"Wait," Jacob said. "How much are you willing to pay me?" He needed it on record that David Huggins was willing to pay him for murder. This was getting better and better every day. Huggins's self-burial.

"One hundred and seventy-five thousand," Huggins whispered. He opened the door to Michael. "You're late, Riley."

Michael ignored his statement, walked past him, and winked at Jacob. "Wassup, brother?" He gave Jacob a hug. He looked over at the senator, finally acknowledging him. "And I know I'm late, David. Do you want me to walk out and come back in again?" He gave him a mock salute.

"I hope you realize that shit you pulled with Ralph Carson cancels out everything," David Huggins hissed.

"What the fuck you talking 'bout?" Mike replied.

"You know he's dead! You know all about it because you called the hit. Do you realize that makes two senators in six months that are dead, murdered right before the Senate vote. Two that opposed me?"

Mike laughed. "Dayum. Sounds like you're in trouble, pal."

"You insufferable piece of shit!" David Huggins screamed.

He lunged at Michael, pushing him hard against the wall. Michael immediately pulled out his gun and pointed it at Huggins's face.

"Are you really that crazy?"

Huggins backed up slowly till he was leaning backward against the arm of his couch. His face read fear.

"You wouldn't shoot me," he whispered.

"Oh, wouldn't I? Bitch, you don't know me."

Michael nodded over to Jacob but kept his eyes on Huggins. "This caucazoid bitch don't know me, does he, brother?"

Jacob hesitated at first and then moved slowly over to Michael. "No, he doesn't. But I know you. You don't want to do this, Mike. It would mess up everything. You can't do this. You're too smart to throw it all away in anger."

"Yeah . . ." Michael pushed the weapon into Huggins's forehead, ignoring Jacob. "Yeah, and that shit about everything being over with? That you calling shit off? That's *bullshit,* you feel me?"

"Mike . . ." Jacob said again.

Michael looked at him, laughed, and put his gun back in his pants front.

"Sorry, brother, I was having a flashback moment."

"Yeah, well, come on back to reality. You can't be threatening our future governor like that. Right, Senator Huggins?"

The senator didn't answer. He was still on his couch's armrest, looking at them both with an as-if look.

The whole game was hilarious to Jacob. He knew that Michael wasn't truly seriously thinking of shooting David Huggins. Not right now at least. To do so would be self-destructive and stupid. And if Michael wasn't anything else, he was intelligent. Jacob had no doubt that Michael planned to keep Huggins under his thumb with threats and eventually blackmail. That's how he operated. The fact that Huggins had mentioned money for murder to Jacob showed that he wasn't unaware of the fact that he would never be free of Michael Riley. Not as long as he breathed air in this world.

Michael looked at Huggins as if he was waiting for some type of response.

"Of course I wasn't really going to hurt my man here," he said. "He knew that." He walked over and flopped down beside Huggins. "So, what are we here for anyhow? Let's talk plans!"

25

Brooklyn, New York

"My God, this car has to be a hundred years old!" Kimberla said as she and Delphi got into the old Maverick Delphi had borrowed from her sister.

"I'm just lucky to have something to get around in," Delphi responded back.

Once they were seated Kimberla fought to buckle the torn seat belt, but finally gave up and sat back with a sigh. "Damn this seat belt!"

"Calm down, Kimberla. It's gonna be okay."

"It's just I feel like I want to kick myself. This doesn't necessarily incriminate me but if it all gets out and anyone discovers that I was the so-called he-she that last saw Carson alive, it could undermine Jacob's alias also."

"Well, keep trying to get him."

All they had been doing for the past two hours was struggling to reach Jacob on his cell phone. He always had it on him and Kimberla couldn't for the life of her figure out why he wasn't answering. There was so much that Jacob had been doing, or rather his attitude and silence toward her, that was confusing.

They were now trying to get to his apartment in record time.

Kimberla hoped he was there chillin' or asleep or something. It didn't matter as long as she got a chance to talk to him and let him know what was going on.

She tried his number one last time as they were pulling up in to his apartment building. Again he didn't answer but they saw him getting into his SUV.

"I've been trying to call you all morning!" Kimberla screamed to him as she approached.

"How are you?"

"How am I? How the hell do you think I am? Man, why have you been avoiding me?"

Jacob pushed her softly against his vehicle. "You need to quiet down. I'm still undercover, Kimmy, and you aren't acting very professional at all." He leaned in close, whispering in her ear.

"Professional?" she gasped out. "I thought we were working as a team, Jacob?"

"No, you were supposed to get your ass out of New York ages ago. And here you are, still here, making trouble. When are you gonna learn that everyone doesn't need Chameleon to figure it all out and make it better, huh?"

"What's going on with you?" Kimberla asked him, shocked by his hostile tone. "Why are you acting this way?"

"Why am I acting this way? Why am I acting this way? You fucking up, girl. That's why!"

"Okay . . . okay." Kimberla put her hands over her face for a second and took a deep breath. "Just listen to me for a second. I know you've had to hear about that senator, Ralph Carson, being found dead, or haven't you?"

"What about that?"

"I was the woman; the so-called he-she that last saw him alive. It's been all over the news. I had to warn you about it, Jacob. Things are getting so crazy and there's so much you don't know . . ."

"No," he said, pointing at her, "there's so much *you* don't know. I've been telling you that all along, but you don't listen. You never listen to anyone, about anything." He quieted at the hurt expression on her face. "Listen . . . I still want you to meet me at three o'clock at Mackings. Don't be late, okay? I'll call you before then and I'll explain everything. I have to go now."

"But what about Carson? I know that Mike had something to do with it, Jacob. He had to. And Carson told me that Senator David Huggins was blackmailing him to change his Senate vote. We have to figure out how all of this is connected. I can help you, Jacob," she pleaded.

Jacob wasn't listening. He got in his vehicle and was closing the door in her face. "I am the one who has to help you now, Kim. Be at Mackings at three. Just trust me, okay?"

"But, Jacob—"

"Be there!"

He started his engine, and pulled off.

Kimberla rushed back to Delphi's car.

"What did he say? What happened?" Delphi asked.

"Follow him. Something is not right. He seemed in a hurry and I want to see where he's going."

Delphi put her hand to her heart. "Lawd have mercy! You folks are gonna drive me insane. I can't take this, Kimberla. I really can't!"

"Just follow him, Delphi!"

En route to warehouse

Jacob prayed to God that Mike hadn't figured out his connection to Kimberla. He looked at his cell phone. Seven missed calls. He flipped it open and all of those calls had been from Kimberla. He jumped when his cell started to ring while still in his hand. Looking at the caller ID, he saw that it was Mike.

"Wassup, Mike?"

"What did she want?"

"Are you behind me?" Jacob asked him, looking in his rear-view mirror.

"Yes, I am, and so is your girl."

Jacob looked at his mirror again and saw an old rangled Maverick following three cars behind. "Damn! I have to lose her," he said to Mike.

"No, to the contrary, this is perfect."

Jacob didn't understand why he could see Kimberla following, along with a woman who appeared to be Delphi, but he couldn't see Mike anywhere.

"What do you mean this is perfect?" he asked him.

"Well . . ." Mike was sucking his teeth in that irritating way he always did. "We are heading to the warehouse right now. All the crew will be there. This is the perfect time for you to get rid of that nosey bird. And with this being an unplanned thing with her, she won't have any backup to protect her. This is the perfect time for you to show me your loyalty. Kill that bitch."

Things couldn't have been worse, Jacob thought. This was not *his* plan. Michael was right: she had no protection and he had no way out of this. Everything was to go down this evening. After today he was finally to be done with the whole sting with Michael Riley. How could he protect Kimberla without blowing his cover prematurely?

His cell phone buzzed. He looked down at the face of it, thinking it would be Kimberla again. Wrong, it was David Huggins. He answered.

"Senator Huggins, hold up one moment please. I have Mike on hold." He clicked the send button. "Mike, I have someone else on the line. I'll call you right back, okay? Are you still behind me somewhere?"

Looking around, Jacob still saw Kimberla creeping close by, but he didn't see Michael.

"Of course I am. I'm like a spider. You never know what hole I may crawl out of." Michael laughed.

"Yeah, okay." Jacob didn't find anything Mike said funny. He could feel his jaw twitching. "Anyhow I really don't think this is the right time to do anything to her. She's not alone in that car."

"I know she's not. Delphi's bitch ass is in there with her. Hmm . . . I guess she's a snitch, too. That's okay though. You take care of your piece of ass, I'll talk care of mine. And we both will come out smelling like roses. Okay, we're getting near the storage house now. I'm gonna go park around the back. Bring her in, brother. Let's do this."

He hung up as Jacob parked his SUV. Jacob took a deep breath, then remembered he had Huggins on the other line. He looked down at his phone. Instead of speaking again with Huggins, he closed his flip. It was all getting to be too damn much.

He got out of his vehicle and locked it. Glancing around, he didn't see Kimberla and Delphi, or Michael Riley. Sweat poured down his face. Jacob wasn't sure if it was the heat of the day or nerves. He got a handkerchief from his back pocket and wiped his face. He was stalling for time. What the fuck was he gonna do? He didn't have the gun he had planned to fill with blanks later that evening. That he had planned to use on Kimberla, or have Michael think he was using it, to kill her. He didn't have the needle filled with the sleep potion he had planned to use on her either, so that Michael would think her dead. There was no protection for either of them at this point. *If we make it out alive, I really will kill her.* Jacob laughed nervously to himself.

After wasting as much time as he could, Jacob slowly walked up to the warehouse. With no Kimberla in sight he prayed that she had been hit by a train. As crazy as that sounded, she would have a better chance of surviving that than what was ahead of her and him if she walked in that warehouse.

26

Crowns Heights, Brooklyn

Kimberla licked her lips, which had gone dry as she pulled into a parking lot that was around the corner from where Jacob had parked. She was not as careless and stupid with this particular assignment as he seemed to think. Something was not right. She could see it in his eyes when they were talking. She could smell it.

"Why do you think he went in there?" Delphi asked her, pointing to the warehouse.

"I don't know."

"Maybe . . . maybe you should just try calling him again?" Delphi looked worried.

"Yeah, maybe I—oh, damn!" Kimberla looked down at her cell phone. The battery had run out. Delphi looked at it also and began to shake her head.

"Let's just leave, Kimberla," she begged.

Thinking hard for a moment, Kimberla said, "How about this—you stay in the car. Give me ten minutes and if I'm not back by then, go and call this number." She grabbed a piece of paper from her purse and scribbled down Malcolm Johnson's number.

Delphi looked at the paper. "Who is this?"

"It's a fellow agent. Just tell him. He'll know what to do."

"Kimberla, please don't go in there."

Kimberla was already walking away.

"Kimberla!"

"Just remember what I said," she screamed back. Kimberla wanted to calm her friend down, but there was nothing else she could say or do but assure Delphi to trust her. "Remember, stay in the car. Ten minutes, I promise!"

The warehouse was full of raw meat on one side and stocked with reduced-price clothing and material on the other. The workers in the clothing part were illegal immigrants employed by Michael Riley. It seemed like there were no illegal operations in the good old USA that Michael didn't have his hands into.

Jacob walked inside, using the key that Michael had given him a year ago to let himself in. The warehouse area masqueraded as a clothing factory, but in reality it was used to store something else—millions of dollars worth of cocaine, crack, heroin, and an assortment of candies, specially made for the city's hardcore junkies. It was also where they were all going to meet.

"Is anyone here?" Jacob called out.

"Hey, come on in the back office, Jonathon," Jacob heard Michael say over the loudspeaker.

He walked past the rows and rows of stockpiled fabrics. Once he got to the back room that he knew Michael used as an office, he opened the door. Michael was alone.

"You got here fast."

"I have many secret entrances," Michael announced proudly. "So, where's your girl?"

"She may not have been following me after all. I didn't see her park anywhere near."

Michael stuck a cherry Blow Pop in his mouth. "Oh she was following you all right. You must have been hitting that ass good for her to be jockin' you like this. Or either she thought she could get some information from you to get to me." He laughed.

"Yeah, whatever," Jacob said dryly. "Either way, it's almost over now. Thank God."

"Yes, thank God." Michael walked over to Jacob and placed his arm on his shoulder. "We are about to make some big dollars, Jonathon. I couldn't have done it without you. You realize that, right?"

Both Michael and Jacob paused when they heard the sound of the doors closing. Jacob's heart began racing and he knew that no matter what, he would have to protect Kimberla, even if it meant blowing the case and his cover.

"There's Miss Chameleon now," Michael said with a smirk spread all over his face.

They walked out to the main entrance and were surprised when, instead of seeing Kimberla, it was Mario Lincoln and Jones. Mario was holding Delphi the dancer with her arms pulled back behind her.

"So did your agent friend abandon you, Delphi?" Michael asked her.

"I-I just came in here by myself. I was looking for you, Michael. I just wanted to find you and talk about what happened. I need work." She was shaking and her face was red. Her lips trembled. Jacob looked around her and the guys. He knew Kimberla had to be hiding somewhere.

"Where is Alisha?" he asked her.

"I don't know . . ." Delphi said in a whisper.

Jacob tried to speak to her with his eyes. He wasn't sure if she was listening. He desperately needed to find out where Kimberla was before Michael did.

"Can I tap her ass before we kill her, Mike?" Jones asked in his typical scum voice.

"No time for that, Jones," Michael said with a laugh. He walked up to Delphi and pulled her face up by her chin. "It's over for you, Delphi. Time's up."

Kimberla took long-legged strides back to Delphi's beat-up Maverick. Delphi had been right. Things were too quiet and with no sign of Jacob, hindsight said to wait.

She got to the car and looked around. There was no Delphi.

"Delphi?" she called out. She looked in the backseat, then on the car floor. "Oh damn, she's hardheaded!"

Kimberla looked in all different directions, but she knew in her heart of hearts that Delphi had gone inside that warehouse. She walked quickly around to the side door. She tested it, and surprisingly it opened with a slight creaking sound. She heard male voices and she paused, leaning flat against the wall so as not to be seen. It was times like this that being skinny and limber came in handy.

"So what did you think you doing? You five-O now, huh?"

Kimberla recognized Michael Riley's voice. Next she heard Delphi.

"I'm not a cop. I don't know what you're talking about. Ooohh! Michael, please!"

Kimberla bit her tongue when Delphi cried out. Someone was slapping her.

"You may not be five-O but you been ratting to them. You think I wouldn't find out what you were up to? Damn, Delphi, don't you know me by now? Don't you know me better than that? Hold her tight, Mario." Michael slapped her again.

"Where is Alisha, Delphi?" It was Jacob.

Kimberla fought hard to keep still and quiet. So Jacob had come in after all. She wondered how he managed to slip in without her seeing him.

"Where is she, Delphi?" Jacob asked her again. "Where is Alisha or Kimberla?"

Huh? Jacob was saying her real name. He was obviously playing a good game for Michael, Mario, and Jones's benefit. Still, it felt odd hearing him talk that way about her around the other guys.

"Y'all know this is a waste of my time. Just shoot her ass," Michael said.

No! Kimberla screamed in her heart. She struggled within to calm down. Jacob was there. He wouldn't let them kill her. She knew he wouldn't. He was a trained agent. He knew what to do. Anytime someone's life was in danger and there was the ability to stop it, a trained agent would do just that, in spite of their alias.

She could still hear Delphi crying, begging for her life. She closed her eyes and prayed that Jacob would do something fast before it was too late.

He won't let them hurt her, Kimberla thought to herself. *He won't—*

She peeked over at them again. Mario was holding Delphi and Jones had a gun pointed right at her. Kimberla's mind started racing. *Why the hell won't Jacob do something?*

"Shoot her ass, Jones," Michael hissed.

"With pleasure," Jones said, laughing.

Reaching into the back panel of her slacks, Kimberla pulled out her gun. She aimed it at Jones. Suddenly a shot rang out, then another. Delphi slumped back against Mario and fell. Kimberla's heart totally stopped when she realized that it was Jacob who had pulled the trigger.

"Whoa!" Michael Riley and Mario Lincoln said in unison.

"I didn't think you had it in you, brother."

Michael patted Jacob on the back as Jacob blew into the barrel of his .38, and smiled.

"Think again," he said. "I never could stand snitching bitches. Now we need to find Alisha and give her the same medicine. Let's leave the body here. I'll get it cleaned up."

The rest of the conversation was a blur of words to Kimberla. She flattened herself against the door and held her hands to her stomach.

"Oh my God!" she whispered to herself. "Oh my God!"

27

Brooklyn, New York

The sun was going down in the Big Apple. Looking out the bus window, every person seemed like an animated clown figure to Kimberla. All with fake smiles, fake lives, and fake people full of lies. Was anyone ever who we truly thought them to be?

Her mind went back to Jacob, the man she thought she knew so well. Special Agent Jacob White. She saw him in her mind and her heart. She saw him with those dark, penetrating eyes; those sexy lips that had made her body burn. Her Georgetown University secret crush. The truth be known he was the only man who had ever touched her heart. But this same man had shot a woman in cold blood.

Why? she cried to herself. Why would he do it? Had he been just another Sebastian Rogers all along? Sebastian was another story, but one that she would never forget. Although they had not always agreed on everything, Kimberla once had great respect for her assistant agent in charge. That was all killed, along with him, when it was found out that he was a dirty agent. That disappointment hardly compared to the pain she felt due to Jacob's betrayal. Why had he done it? Had the money Michael was making seduced Jacob that much, the way he had seduced her heart and her body? What made a good agent turn bad?

Kimberla sniffed and took a deep breath. She wiped away the ribbons of tears that had been trailing down her cheeks from the moment she had gotten on the bus, knowing that Michael Riley, and especially Jacob, would assume she'd take the train. They would also assume she'd be going back to her apartment, and through the front entrance, but she might not be able to fool Jacob so easily. Kimberla felt damned that he knew her too well.

Here is another lesson learned, she thought; *another key to being a good undercover agent. Never let anyone, even other agents, know your routine too well. You never truly know who is good and who is bad. You never know who is on your side and who is simply a greedy opportunist.*

Creeping in from the alley entrance, Kimberla took her pistol out and unlocked her back door. She walked in cautiously. Everything was extremely quiet, but just to be sure she knocked over the cactus plant that sat on the end table. It flew noisily against the wall. If someone was in her apartment they would be in for the fight of their lives.

So far she seemed to be the only one there. She searched her apartment room-by-room till she determined that she was solo. After that she got to packing.

Kimberla had hated taking a chance coming back there, but with the job she had ahead of her she needed some of her things.

There were many ways she could bust Michael's enterprise. But the most important thing right now was for her to get back to the warehouse and see if Delphi's body was still there. Then she would go to Mackings and take a look in Michael's office. Kimberla knew that Michael had his new club opening this night, and she also knew what a money hog he was. He wouldn't cancel that based on the events of the day. An arrest of Michael

Riley at his opening would humiliate him and show him to be the lizard that he was. She knew any pertinent information Michael had on Senator David Huggins was at his Mackings office, though.

She hadn't forgotten the real reason she was in New York— to make sure that Margo's killers were brought to justice. All of them! David Huggins was first on that list. His hands were dirtied not just with Margo's blood, but Benita James, Ronnie Jones, and even Ralph Carson's in a roundabout way.

Just as she was packing the last of the clothing and equipment that she would need to bring this job to a finish, her house phone rang. She froze, wondering if she should answer. Something told her it was Jacob.

She walked slowly over to the phone and picked it up. She didn't say hello, she didn't say anything.

"Kimberla?" Jacob whispered after her moment's pause. "I know this is you. Listen carefully, okay?"

"You dirty muthafucka . . ."

"Look, shut the hell up and listen!" he stormed, still in a whispered tone.

Kimberla wasn't hearing him. She felt as if every bone in her body were about to crack from pain, anger, disappointment, and shock. Jacob was a dirty agent. That was the only thought permeating her distraught mind.

"I don't wanna listen to you," she said. "There is nothing you can say, Jacob. You are worse than the criminals you were assigned to bring down. You are nothing, and you are the one that's going down. I promise you this."

"It's not what you saw," he whispered. "Delphi is not, she's not—"

"Was that bullet meant for me? You meant to kill me didn't you, Jacob?"

Jacob sighed. "Yes, it was meant for you, and no I didn't mean to kill you. It's not what you think you saw, Kimberla. I had to do that. I had to make Mike believe it. But Delphi is not—"

"You bitch muthafucka you . . . It's not over. Have you forgotten who I am? It's not over by a long shot."

She was about to hang up the phone when she heard . . . "Just go to the warehouse. Go now while the workers are there. She's not dead, Kimberla. Delphi is not dead!"

28

Crown Heights

"Are you new?" a woman asked with a strong accent.

Kimberla didn't answer her at first. She looked at the woman as if she were confused and kept working.

"Can you talk, young man?" the woman said again.

Kimberla turned to her and said, "Yes," in a deep, adolescent voice.

The woman had called her young man because that's how Kimberla was dressed. She wore baggie blue jeans that hung low on her narrow hips, a large T-shirt, and Timberland boots. She had bound her breasts, which were small anyway, so that she appeared flat, and she wore big glasses that she hoped concealed her femininity a bit.

Michael always had the factory open for business three nights a week. Fortunately none of the people who worked for Mackings were around because even in her homeboy wear, Kimberla figured that someone she had been seeing on a day-to-day basis would recognize her. She knew she had taken a risk listening to Jacob after what she had witnessed.

Why did he say Delphi wasn't dead? Why did he want her to come back here? And the biggest question, why did she still trust him? Or was there something inside her that knew all along that what she was seeing with her very own eyes could not be the Jacob she had always known?

Even with everything that was going on, the little fears she held inside about her feelings for Jacob would not dissipate; her feelings wouldn't either. She didn't know for sure if getting her to come to the warehouse was a setup, but she prayed for the sake of her life and the sake of her heart that it wasn't.

"Bathroom," Kimberla suddenly said to the woman who had been addressing her.

The woman smiled. "Okay, hurry. We have much work to do."

Kimberla rushed to the bathrooms toward the loading area. The door was locked. Jacob had told her to go there but before he completed his sentence he had been cut off or had hung up. This was so unlike her. She never took chances or walked into a situation blind.

She shook the door yet still it wouldn't budge.

"Hmph," she said aloud to herself. She knew there had to be another entrance.

She walked around to the side delivery door and it too was locked. *Damn Jacob! What the fuck was she looking for?*

She looked at her watch. She had to get back to the front before the nosey woman came looking for her. She reached back and rubbed her neck. Mental exhaustion was taking its toll, but she didn't have time to worry about that.

She turned and then suddenly she heard voices and the sound of the back door opening. She caught her breath and waited. After the two men who had been talking went by, she made her move. Something told her that if Delphi was alive, as Jacob had said, she was in that back room.

Kimberla tiptoed inside, but shock of shocks, it wasn't the injured body of Delphi lying on the floor, but rows and rows of packed cocaine. It was neatly packed and squared. She blinked at the sight of it. This wasn't a labor warehouse. This was where Michael Riley stored his drug products. Is this what Jacob wanted her to see? Why did he make her think that Delphi would be here? Kimberla was feeling even more confused.

She took out her small camera and started snapping pictures. As she turned to make her way out she bumped into a hard chest. Looking upward she caught her breath. It was Jones . . .

"Fuck you taking pictures for, boy?" he spat.

Words seem to be stuck in Kimberla's throat. She was caught. She looked around anxiously.

"You hear me talking to you? What you doing here and what do you have that camera for?"

He suddenly got a good look at her. "Alisha?"

Kimberla wasn't the sitting-duck type. She moved fast, clipping Jones in the gut with her knee. He fell immediately to his knees and she ran, heading for the side door past the storage of cocaine. She found herself in a room with no other doors but the one she had just entered. Damn, she thought.

"Where are you, Alisha?" Jones called out to her. "I hope you know there's nowhere to go hide in here."

Kimberla heard the door creak open and stooped down behind a stack of cocaine. She held her breath as she slowly took her pistol from her back belt. She double-checked to make sure the silencer was tight, and cocked it. She could still hear Jones laughing in a hyena fashion.

"You know, Alisha, I should just lock ya ass in here and give da boss a call. But then on second thought that would be stupid. I've been wanting to get me of a taste of you for a long time, baby. So why don't you stop this hide and seek game and come to daddy." He laughed again.

Kimberla held her gun close to her chest. *Come on, fool,* she thought, *come and get me.* She knew she would have to take Jones out of this world tonight if she wanted to get out alive.

She suddenly saw him standing in the shadows, smack in front of her.

"Gotcha!" Jones taunted. He aimed a small handgun toward her head.

She fired. Jones stepped back two feet as Kimberla stood up, looking him dead in the eye. He started pulling at his shirt, yanking at the buttons as if he hadn't even been hit.

"What the fuck? What the hell?" he whispered in surprise. He looked up at her. "You shot me."

"I sure did." She raised her eyebrow. "I'm your worst nightmare, bitch."

He raised his pistol and lunged for her, screaming out obscenities. She fired again, cutting his words in half. This time Jones fell back hard against the wall. He blinked once, twice, then stilled.

Kimberla looked at him lying there and shook her head. Somehow it never bothered her when she had to take out a dangerous criminal, and this time was no different.

She unscrewed the silencer from her gun and calmly put it back in the safe spot of her jeans.

"Kimberla . . ."

Kimberla jumped at the sound of her named moaned out. She looked up and there was Delphi, standing at the opened door. Her shirt and shoulder were bloodied.

"Oh, Delphi, I thought Jacob had killed you!" she whispered, rushing over to help her friend.

"No." Delphi leaned back against the door, tired from the blood loss. "He told me to hide in the closet. He told me he would be sending you back for me. You took so long!"

Kimberla checked Delphi's shoulder. It was mainly a surface wound but still bled heavily. It then hit her what Jacob had done—what he had been trying to tell her on the phone. By shooting Delphi, he had saved her life.

"I saw him shoot you twice, girl. I know he did." Delphi shook her head weakly as Kimberla asked, "What?"

Kimberla gasped as Delphi showed her the spot over her heart where Jacob had shot. The bullets had been blanks. The relief Kimberla felt made her weak. She should have trusted him all along. The heart never lies, but the eyes do. Her mother had always told her that. Now she understood what those words meant. *Damn, he was a good-ass shot.*

"Did Jacob tell you where he would be? Where they were going?"

"The opening for In Brandy's Corner is tonight. It's Michael's new club in Manhattan. He said that is where they will be. He said you would know what to do; who to call," Delphi responded. She winced in pain. "Kimberla, I need to get to the hospital."

A foreign voice interrupted them.

"Why are you back here?"

It was the lady who had called Kimberla "young man."

Kimberla pulled her FBI badge from her pocket, and her gun. "FBI," she said to the woman in her natural voice. "Where's a telephone?"

The woman drew back in shock. "What—what?"

"Look, this woman has been shot and there's a dead body over there underneath all those packs of pure cocaine. You're not in any trouble but this place is going to be under surveillance. We need to get an ambulance for her. Trust me, you don't want to get mixed up in this. I need a telephone before any of the bad people find out we're here. Are you going to help me?"

The woman shook her head violently. "Yes, yes! I don't know anything about bad men, please, I don't."

"I know you don't," Kimberla said, seeing the trembles in the woman's bottom lip. She felt remorse at having scared her and put her gun down to calm the woman. "Just take me to a telephone."

She looked at Delphi who was still trembling in pain against the door. "I need to call Malcolm."

"Who's Malcolm?" Delphi asked her.

"He's one of our men from D.C. But listen, I don't want you to worry about anything, okay?" She put her arms around Delphi. "Everything's gonna be all right, girl. Everything's gonna be all right."

29

Manhattan, New York

Michael was in full celebratory mood. Dressed in white from head to toe, he stood out in the crowd, the way he always wanted to.

Jacob stood not far behind him, trying to think up a feasible answer to the question he had just been asked. Michael asked him again.

"Well? What exactly did you do with the body?"

He lit a cigar, blew the flickering flames out, and waited patiently for Jacob's reply.

"After you guys left I dragged it to the freezer, then I went to see if Alisha was anywhere to be found," Jacob stated. "I told you I'd take care of it, man."

"What?" Michael stormed. "Why would you leave the body there when you knew our workers were coming in at six? Not to mention the fact that your agent is still out there."

"She's not my agent. Again you keep forgetting that you hired her."

"Whatever." He waved his cigar roughly. "She's probably been trying to contact the feds, although I know she hasn't as of yet."

"How do you know that?" Jacob asked. He was getting a weird feeling about Michael. The only thing that seemed to be on his mind right now was where Delphi's body was. Not the fact that his organization was spotlighted by the feds or that Kimberla was an agent herself.

"Because I checked."

"You checked?"

Michael laughed. "Do you really think I got as far as I have by being stupid, Jonathon? I knew about Alisha for the past week. Lia found out around the same time, but I have other sources. Do you really think David Huggins is only around to help us get through customs?"

"But you seemed so surprised and angry when you told me about it," Jacob said in confusion.

"I had to know I could trust you, brother. That thing with Delphi, though, was not supposed to happen. Alisha, well I'm not even worried about her. As soon as she contacts her source, she's dead. Hold up," he said, as his phone rang.

His words made Jacob catch his breath. Something was wrong. He had somehow underestimated Mike and that was something he never did with anyone.

"—so where is she heading?"

Jacob caught the last part of Michael's conversation and woke up from his thoughts.

"Well listen, tell your man to go there and act like everything is normal. Tell her the feds have me in custody, something like that. I'll have someone waiting at the door for her when she leaves. What? No, nobody needs to be inside, David. The less your cop friends know, the better, and the more people who know about shit the more bodies we're gonna have to burn."

Fuck, Jacob thought, it never failed. Mike and David Huggins had someone working with them from within the Bureau—someone Kimberla obviously trusted.

"Look," Michael continued. "Don't blame me for this shit. If you had your people on top of things from the start none of this would have happened. That shit with the white chick, that other agent wouldn't have happened either. Just do what the fuck you need to do and tell your snoop not to let her get to NYPD or any other agent that's clean and legit! Now I have to go and open my club. Take care of business on your end, muthafucka." He slammed the phone down and turned to look at Jacob.

"What's wrong, why you looking at me like that?" he asked.

"What was that?"

"David Huggins."

"You have federal agents on your payroll." Jacob said this as a statement, not a question.

"Nope. David Huggins does. And I have Huggins in my pocket. Ingenious, isn't it?" Michael winked.

Kimberla didn't know what was taking Malcolm so long. She had called him over a half hour ago and still no show. She also told him about Delphi and told him to call an ambulance. He was pigheaded, and as far as she was concerned, incompetent in a lot of things, but this tardiness in such a dire situation was not like him at all.

"What's taking them so long, Kimberla?" Delphi moaned.

Kimberla looked at her and sighed. She knew Delphi had been in pain a long time. Even if her wound was surface, the pain and blood lost could put her in shock if an ambulance didn't get there soon.

They were with the line leader—the woman that had took to the employee break room to use the phone. The woman still looked scared and shaken.

"I'm gonna call the ambulance myself," Kimberla said.

She got up slowly and walked over to the telephone, picked it up and again dialed Malcolm's number. It rang and rang and there was no answer. She placed the phone back on its receiver and walked out of the room, pacing.

"I'll be right back," she said.

She walked out to the loading area and leaned against the wall, holding her breath in and then letting it out slowly. *What was she gonna do?*

"What room did he say she was in?" a masculine voice suddenly said.

"The door is open here. She's over here," came another whisper. "Take her out?"

Kimberla jumped. *Take her out?* She thought as she heard the voices that it was the NYPD and ambulance finally coming for them. But a little voice in her head said to stay quiet. She pulled her pistol out and turned to peek around the corner. As she turned there was a storm of automatic gunshot fire and screams as two men attacked the foreign line leader and Delphi in the break room. Kimberla cried inside as she heard it. Delphi may not have been dead before, but she was for sure dead now.

After getting over the initial shock of what was happening, Kimberla put her arm around the corner, aimed, and started firing. One guy caught a bullet on the side of his face, and fell hard against his partner. His partner gasped as blood splattered into his face and then used his dead friend's body as a shield when Kimberla kept firing. He fired back, coating the wall that protected her with bullets. She quietly waited, measuring her next step. She wasn't sure if her bullets had landed or not, but she wasn't taking any chances.

Kimberla reached down to her ankle and pulled out her throwaway, .25 automatic that she kept for possible moments like this. She looked cautiously around the corner. A bullet flew past her head, barely missing her. She knew she had to get out of the warehouse completely if she was to have a chance. Throwing caution to the wind, Kimberla screamed as she turned the corner and started firing with both pistols, running as she did so. Luck was with her. The guy who had been spooking her out didn't even have a moment to fire back. He fell back against the break-room door with his eyes wide open. Blood trickled down the corner of his mouth.

Kimberla stepped up and kicked him to be sure he was dead. She reached down into his pants pocket and grabbed his keys and cell phone. If God was with her she wouldn't have too hard a time finding the car belonging to the two men. She looked into the break room. Delphi was sprawled across the table. Her shirt was fully red, and her body was still, as was the poor woman, the line leader who had helped them.

I don't have time to cry yet, Kimberla thought. She would cry tomorrow. Today, at this moment, she had to get to Michael Riley's new club. There was no doubt in her mind that Malcolm Johnson had set her and Delphi up. What was also clear in her mind was that by her telling Malcolm that she needed an ambulance for Delphi, Jacob's cover was now blown. He was in danger and didn't even know it.

Kimberla walked quickly from the back room to the clothing line. Both her guns were still in her hands. It was odd, but even with the shooting that the immigrant workers had obviously heard, none of them had moved. It was as if they were programmed to ignore every shady activity around them.

She walked out of the warehouse and spotted two vehicles: a Ford Navigator and a small sport BMW. She looked down at the keys and found a Ford key. She climbed into the Navigator and started it up. Yes, God was with her.

There was nothing but wind and dirt behind as Kimberla pulled off, heading for Michael Riley's new club. She only hoped that God would also be with Jacob, and that she would get to him before it was too late.

30

Jacob needed getaway time, but that was something he just didn't have. There was a fine line to be drawn when it came to doing whatever it took to hold your cover and doing whatever it took to save your life and the lives of your fellow agents. But Kimberla Bacon wasn't just his fellow agent, she was the second woman in his life who had grabbed his heart and she didn't even know it.

Michael had assigned him to stand guard by the stage with Mario Lincoln, while he, Michael, introduced the club to the happy, horny patrons.

Jacob patted his chest, feeling for the Uzi automatic that was buckled inside his coat lining; he also checked his back jean loop for the tech .9 pistol that was hooked there. He took a deep breath, then looked over at Mario.

"Yo, I need to take a leak. Can you be four eyes for a few minutes?"

"Don't take long," Mario whispered back, "you know how Mike be trippin' about security."

"He still pissed 'cause Jones ain't back."

Jacob looked around the busy dance hall, noting that it was

getting very crowded. He needed to get NYPD there as soon as possible before too much chaos erupted once Michael found out who he was. And for sure as soon as he had help in place he was more than ready to finally make that bust. He only hoped Kimberla was okay . . .

Mario looked at Jacob. "You in a fuckin' daze, nigga. Wassup wit' you? I thought you had to piss?"

"I-I do," Jacob stammered. He felt this sudden wind of nerves hit him. But it wasn't a wind. It was the women who had come onstage after Michael's introduction. One of them was so very familiar. One of them brought heat, happiness and fear to Jacob's heart. He knew right away that the woman with the Arabia silk veil and piercing eyes was none other than Kimberla Bacon.

Jacob's attention went back to Mario who was looking at him questioningly. "I'll be right back," he said.

Michael Riley left the stage at the same time as Jacob did. Jacob watched as he walked toward the back offices and disappeared behind closed doors. He backed up into the men's bathroom, checked all the stalls to see if he was alone, then closed himself inside of one to call NYPD. When he opened the flip of his phone he noted that there were two missed calls. He listened to his voice mail.

"Jacob, it's Kimberla. I know you didn't kill Delphi now. I'm so sorry I ever allowed myself to believe you would ever do anything like that. But she's dead now," she cried.

"What?" Jacob said out loud.

"But you have to listen to me carefully," her voice mail continued. *"You have to hold out till I get to Brandy's. Watch your back and get away from Michael if you can. I couldn't bear if anything happened to you, Jacob . . . I, well I pray to God one day I can tell you just how I feel."* She took a deep breath. *"Just watch your back. I'm on my way."*

What is she talking so crazy about? he thought. He continued to listen to the voice mail.

"Jacob, they know, they—"

The door to the bathroom stall opened up. Jacob closed his

phone lid quickly. His eyes widened as two of Michael Riley's men stood outside the door giving him a hard look.

"Boss wants to talk to you," one of them said. Jacob recognized him to be Jimmy Main, small-time bouncer that Michael used at times when he wanted to rough someone up.

"What—what do you mean?" Jacob asked, trying to stay calm. "Can I finish pissing first?"

He hadn't even blinked before there was a fat black .9 millimeter poking in his temple.

"I just said, boss wanna talk to you. Now move the fuck on."

He had recognized her even in her sexy Arabia wear.

Kimberla wanted and needed to get inside the club without too many people noticing her. To pull it off she came in from the back with the other dancers.

As she was walking offstage, after the "welcome to In Brandy's Corner dance," she frowned, thinking about the poor, brown-skinned chick she'd had to knock out so that she could take her place in the dance. It paid off, however. Jacob had recognized her and she was assured that he was okay. Now she only had to lay low until NYPD got there.

It was so sad that Malcolm's jealousy of her had made him go down to the level of setting her up and trying to get her killed. She couldn't help but wonder if he had anything to do with Margo's murder. He obviously knew Michael or David Huggins—someone inside the whole dirty situation.

Kimberla sighed as her thoughts begin to run into each other. She walked to a small room that was actually beside the dressing room, where she had placed her bag of clothes beneath a desk, along with the poor, knocked-out dancer.

After changing back into her toy-boy gear, she crunched down in a corner and took out the cell phone she had stolen from the man she'd killed at the warehouse, and she dialed Jacob's cell.

*   *   *

His cell phone rang relentlessly. But with his arms held tightly behind his back, Jacob couldn't answer, and he really didn't want to. But something told him it was Kimberla calling back.

Jimmy Main and his friend, someone that Jacob didn't recognize, stood over him. They had tied him tightly to the iron chair that was burning into his back. He stared back at Jimmy fearlessly. At this point there wasn't time to be scared, although he had reason to be. He had to find a way to get out of the situation.

The door opened. In walked Mario Lincoln, and behind him, Michael Riley. Mike looked over at Jimmy's friend.

"Go back out and oversee the stage acts," he told him.

When the door closed only Michael, Jimmy, Mario, and Jacob were left in the room. Mike still had not looked at him, but Jacob could feel the explosive chemistry brimming.

He didn't want to look at Mike or Mario. Not that he was afraid of either of them, but he had worked in close quarters with both for a long time. This was not how he had originally planned to bring them down.

"Why, Jonathon?" he heard Mike ask. Pain brought the tenor of his voice down to a whisper.

Jacob cleared his throat. "Why what?" He looked up at Mike with clear eyes. Mike had a notepad in his hand and was reading it quietly.

"So you the feds, huh?" Mario sneered. "Can't believe all this time. You walking around like you a bad muthafucka and you just a paid snitch."

Jacob was still silent, which seemed to incense Mario even more. He rushed over to Jacob and pulled him by the collar.

"I always knew something was fucked up about you. I always knew!" He threw him back against the chair. "Let me smoke 'em, Mike!"

"Get back," Mike suddenly said, putting his hand on Mario's arm. He moved closer to Jacob. "You know what bothers me the most about all this, Jonathon? It's not that you're an agent. That's your career choice and I guess somebody has to do it. It's that you had me so convinced that you were real; that you cared about our friendship, our brotherhood. All the time it was a con to help the white man bring down a brotha. You didn't have to go that far. I'm not close to all my men, the way I was with you. You didn't have to go that far . . ."

He moved his hands to both sides of Jacob's face and bent down till they were nose to nose. Then he hugged him hard.

"You broke my heart, brother." He squeezed his cheeks hard and shook Jacob. "You broke my heart!"

Michael walked away, not even looking at Mario and Jimmy Main as he whispered, "Three slugs, to the head. Use a silencer and make sure he's dead . . ."

She had to find Jacob. Kimberla tried hard to compose herself, as she listened to the ring of Jacob's cell phone, and still no answer. She imagined all kinds of things that could have happened to him. What if he was dead? Her heart quivered at the thought. She couldn't stand it; she couldn't sit and wait any longer.

The door to the storage room made a creaking sound as she opened it. No matter the danger she would search the whole damn club until she found her man. That's right, she said it, *her* man. At this point the idea of it didn't scare her one tiny bit.

The hallway was empty. She took a deep breath and walked quietly alongside the wall. There were footsteps coming! The sound of them made Kimberla's heart jump and she turned into the first door she came to.

Shit! She was in the women's dressing room. It was set up almost exactly like the one at Mackings, bathroom stalls and all. Fortunately it appeared to be empty.

"Bitch, what are you doing still alive?"

The voice that spat those words was clearly recognizable.

Lia Chamberlayne.

31

Manhattan, New York

Lia had a knife, and was wheeling it around as she spoke. Kimberla almost laughed, thinking of how easy it would be to make her eat that knife.

"Your hoe-ass is supposed to be dead. What the hell! You got nine lives or sumpin?"

Kimberla was sick of Lia's trouble-making ass; sick of her. She put her hands up as if in surrender and walked over to her slowly.

"This is police business, Lia. In five minutes this place is gonna be crawling with NYPD and federal agents. Now you don't have to like me, but you don't want to be mixed up in this any more than you already are."

Lia almost snarled at her. "Why did you come here? Messing with Jonathon; trying to get Michael in trouble. Why couldn't you have stayed where you were?"

They circled around each other. Lia naively kept thrusting her pocketknife at Kimberla as if she wasn't quite sure she could take her.

Good, Kimberla thought. She should be nervous. Kimberla didn't have time to play games with her though. Time was ticking away and she had to find Jacob. She also didn't want to take a chance of another dancer coming in the room.

"Put it down, Lia. This is your last warning." She smiled at her. "You have no idea how bad I'd love to whip your ass. So I suggest you put that knife down before . . ."

She hadn't quite gotten the words out before Lia was coming at her with a vengeance. Lia wasn't fast enough. As soon as she got close enough for Kimberla to reach her hand out, Kimberla kicked the knife out of her hand. Lia screamed. Alarmed and worried that someone had heard the scream, Kimberla jump-kicked Lia again, this time landing a right foot to her chest. The kick sent Lia flying backward against the door, making a loud, thumping noise, knocking Lia out in a flash.

"Oh damn! I don't know my own strength sometimes," Kimberla said.

She jumped when she heard the sound of someone running in the hallway. After looking around in desperation, she found a place to hide.

Leaving Jacob under the watchful eye of their boss, Mario Lincoln and Jimmy Main rushed to see where the noise had come from, per Michael's request. Mario figured the noise had come from the women's dressing room, and ran in that direction. He pushed the door open.

"Dayum," he exclaimed, "what happened here?"

Lia was laid out flat on the floor, her eyelids flickering. Jimmy Main reached down and checked her pulse.

"She's alive," he said. He noticed that Mario was looking in another direction with his gun drawn, so he quickly did the same. Jimmy Main saw Kimberla on top of the bathroom stall and squeezed off a shot. He felt a hot, burning sting to his chest. He heard another shot, but didn't feel anything. Only the weight of his body falling as he saw Mario Lincoln falling also.

Kimberla hopped down from the top of the bathroom stalls. The height leverage gave her a perfect bird's-eye view when the two men came in.

"And look at you now," she whispered to their dead bodies. She stepped over them and walked outside of the dressing room. All Kimberla could think of was that she had to find Jacob. Not later, but now. She kept her gun out and walked down the hall, checking every room as she went.

"Stay right there, Alisha."

Kimberla turned around at the sound of Michael Riley's voice. He had Jacob in front of him and a huge .9 millimeter pointed to the back of his head. Jacob gave Kimberla a nervous look. His eyes held strength though, and they helped strengthen her resolve.

"Michael . . ."

Michael looked around himself crazily and pushed the gun harder into the back of Jacob's head.

"Michael?" Kimberla whispered again. "They're gonna be coming for you. You don't want to shoot him. You don't want to add to the list of your crimes. Please put the gun down . . ." She held her own gun steadily.

Michael looked at her with a crazed expression. He was almost laughing.

"The list of my crimes? Sister, you have no idea the list of crimes that's been committed against me." He pushed his knee into Jacob's back, causing him to give a painful grunt, but still Jacob stood there bravely. "What about niggas who claim to be your brother? What about brothers who claim to be your nigga? Your boy? You, all of you are just a bunch of sold-out muthafuckas, fighting for the white man. You think they care about you?"

Kimberla fought not to blink when she saw two SWAT officers creeping up behind Michael and Jacob. She needed to keep Michael's attention directed on her in order to keep Jacob alive. Jacob spoke before she could.

"You prey on your own people, Mike," he said with disgust. "That makes you the sold-out brotha. Not me. Those drugs you feed into poor neighborhoods? You prey on your own people. So don't fuckin' preach to me, preach to yourself. You ain't nothing but a killer."

"I ain't never gave a nigga nothing who didn't have it coming!"

"Shit, man. Who didn't have it coming? You don't care about
human lives. You'll kill a woman like you poppin' off birds.
You killed your other flesh and blood—your own brother!"

Michael lost it, and popped Jacob on the back of the head
with the butt of his gun. Jacob fell like a log to the floor. Michael's
face turned almost scarlet in rage.

"Shut the fuck up! Shut the fuck up! You don't know, nigga."
He pointed his gun at Jacob and released the safety. "You don't
know! I'm Michael Riley. I'm the king in this bitch! You don't
know!"

Bingo, Kimberla thought. She dropped to the floor and closed
her eyes seconds before the SWAT officers opened fire on Michael.
Michael fell to the floor; his body jerked as bullets rumbled
through him.

When the smoke cleared the hallway was flooded with police officers and the SWAT team. Kimberla exhaled in relief and
crawled over to Jacob. He was bent over Michael, who amazingly was still alive and alert.

He took Michael in his arms, looking down at him sadly.
"You know what's crazy?" Michael coughed out weakly.
Blood was drizzling slowly from the corner of his mouth. "I
still got nothing but love for you, brother—nothing but love . . ."
He looked over at Kimberla. "Take care of that sweet th-thing."

Pain and regret coated Jacob's face as Michael took a last
breath, and expired.

The center was filled with cheering senators, congressmen,
and lobbyists. Senator David Huggins smiled gleefully at the response of his words. He'd won. He finally won the nomination
to run for governor of the great state of New York even though
it had come with blood, sweat, and tears. As far as he was concerned the ending justified the means.

David Huggins was a winner. He knew all along this would
be the outcome, with or without Michael Riley's help. He

shook inside as he thought about him. He still had to figure out a way to get rid of the shiftless, black bastard.

"Thank you, thank you!" he shouted to the cheering audience. He raised both hands, fingers making a "V" for victory. He turned away from the audience and smiled at his fellow politicians who patted him on the back and shook his hand as he made his way backstage.

"Hello, Senator Huggins."

David paused at the eyes that glared back at him. Jonathon Simmons. What the hell was he doing here? What the hell was Mike Riley trying to prove?

"What are you doing here?" he whispered viciously.

"I came to watch you make a fool of yourself," Jacob said with a sly smile. "Oh, and one more thing." He pulled out a set of handcuffs. Behind him walked up two plainclothes police officers and a tall black woman.

"You have the right remain silent," Jacob began. "You have a right to an attorney. If you cannot afford one, one will be provided for you."

David Huggins's lips began to tremble. His heart beat rapidly in his chest as he slowly felt the floor weakening beneath his feet. His hands were cuffed behind him as the back hall was flooded with reporters' flashing cameras and senators' shocked expressions.

"Why? Why?" he cried. "Oh, God, I'm innocent. I didn't do anything!"

Jacob laughed, shaking his head at the pitiful look of Huggins. "How about drug trafficking? How about the murder of Agent Margo Hunter, Benita James, Senator Alan Mitchell, and Ronnie Jones? Not to mention you offered to pay me to knock off Michael Riley. Who by the way is dead right now. But don't worry. I have enough tapes and evidence to put you away for a long, long time."

David Huggins was crying outright by now. "Please, please, I didn't have anything to do with it, I'm innocent I tell you! I'm innocent!"

"Well, Senator, you're just one innocent, muthafuckin' governor-to-be. I'm sure you can afford a wonderful attorney. You're gonna need one."

Jacob nodded at the police officers who held Huggins. "Take him outta here."

Kimberla walked up to Jacob. He looked at her and smiled. "Damn, that felt good," he said.

Kimberla's grin got wider in agreement, and then in perfect unison they gave each other a high-five.

EPILOGUE

Bahamas

The water was clear, blue, and beautiful. It bubbled like a heated fountain as Kimberla stepped into it. She sighed at the warmth.

She was finally on vacation. Lawd have mercy Jesus, she deserved it! The job of a secret agent was a hard one. One of the reasons she was happy to give up undercover work was that it was not only emotionally taxing, but physically also. Secretly she enjoyed it, and knew she always would.

She wasn't sure what she was going to do when she got back to D.C. Kyte Williams had asked her that question and it went unanswered. She had gone to New York for a purpose, to find Margo. A knot tightened her throat. Sadly that wasn't to be. But who could question what the Almighty allowed? The most important thing was that she had gotten her friend justice, and justice was what it was all about. Pursuit of justice is the reason both of them had joined the FBI in the first place.

Justice hadn't found Malcolm Johnson, however. He seemed to have disappeared off the face of the earth. That would haunt Kimberla forever. But every dog has its day, and if she had anything to do with it, one day Malcolm would get his.

"Have any room for me in there?"

Kimberla looked up at the deep voice that woke her from her thoughts. Jacob was a sexy somebody, standing there with a thick towel wrapped around his hips and a twinkle in his eye.

"I can make room," she said seductively.

He dropped the towel as he walked over to the hot tub. His dark manhood stuck out boldly as he stepped inside.

Lawd, Kimberla thought, *the brotha is piping. What is he doing so hard?* She licked her lips as he sat down into the water.

"You can't keep your eyes off me, can you?" Jacob laughed.

"Whatever, man." Kimberla flushed in embarrassment.

"C'mere," Jacob coaxed. He pulled her back against him, then moved his hands up her stomach to her breasts as he kissed her neck lightly. Kimberla started laughing.

"What you laughing for, girl? I'm trying to make love with you here."

"I know, I know. I'm just thinking about the look on David Huggins's face when you arrested him. You know that look should make the *Guinness Book of World Records* for most dumbfounded!"

"Yeah, it was funny, but he deserved it."

"And so did Michael Riley?"

Jacob sighed. "You know, Mike is a hard one. He deserved what he got. But it's weird working undercover, getting to know these crooks, and almost starting to like them, or at least some qualities about them. I think in his own mixed-up way Mike didn't see anything wrong in what he was doing."

"And what about you?"

"Me? I'm an agent, doing my job."

"So, um . . ." Kimberla turned around and wrapped her long legs around Jacob's waist. "Why don't you do your job right now, Agent White?" She licked at his eyelashes, flicking her tongue at the edge.

"So are you my woman now?"

"I'm my own woman. You know this."

Jacob pushed her back slightly, frowning. "Why you gotta be so hard?"

"Why can't you just stop with the possessive crap and show me some make-my-toes-curl lovin'?"

Jacob faked a shiver. "Damn, I love it when you nasty."

"Sho you right!" Kimberla laughed, and covered his mouth with hers.